# Love's Compass
## Book Five
# Finding Joy

Melanie D. Snitker

i

Finding Joy (Love's Compass: Book 5)

Published by
**Dallionz Media, LLC**
P.O. Box 643
Boerne, TX 78006

**Cover Design by: Covers and Cupcakes**
https://coversandcupcakes.wordpress.com/

For permission requests, please contact the author at the e-mail below or through her website.

Melanie D. Snitker
melanie@melaniedsnitker.com
www.melaniedsnitker.com

This is a work of fiction. Names, characters, businesses, places, events, and incidents either are the products of the author's imagination or used in a fictitious manner. Any resemblance to actual persons, living or dead, or actual events is purely coincidental.

For Mom and Dad. Thank you
for providing a childhood that inspired
creativity and a home full of happiness and love.

# Prologue

When Parker Wilson's eyes opened, he expected to see the familiar walls of his apartment. Or the curtains filtering the early morning sun coming through the window.

It was dark with only a few slivers of light cutting into the black. What time was it? Had his alarm sounded? He didn't remember turning it off.

He tried to shift positions so he could see his clock sitting on the side table. But the moment he did so, pain bolted through his body and into his head.

A groan worked its way out to fill the surrounding space. All at once, the realization he wasn't lying on his bed at home crashed into him like a tidal wave. A heavy weight pushed against his chest as though it were an ounce away from crushing him. He shoved against it to no avail. What started as a peripheral sensation became searing pain along the right side of his body. Everything hurt. It was impossible to decipher where he was actually injured.

Hot air mixed with an acrid smell and followed the

path to his lungs with each struggling breath. He had to get out. Now!

Sounds of metal bending and squealing exploded in his head. Parker tried to cover his ears to block out the noise, but raising his arms higher than his heart was impossible.

What was happening?

The air around him grew heavy with heat and Parker gulped against the combination of bile and panic rising in his throat.

*God, save me!*

# Chapter One
## *One Year Later*

Parker lurched upright in bed, his chest heaving and sweat trickling down the sides of his face. The bedroom was still semi-dark as the sun peeked over the horizon, ushering in another chilly day in central Texas. He raised a hand and felt his right cheek. His fingers followed the grooves of the scars that ran from his eyebrow, cut close to his ear, and ended just above the carotid artery in his neck. That his carotid remained intact was the only reason he'd survived the car wreck. A fact many doctors at the hospital had made a point of telling him. Others insisted it was the grace of God. That it was a second chance at life and he should make the best of it.

Considering his entire life had come crashing down that night, maybe God should've picked another candidate. Bitterness ran through his veins, mirroring the way even deeper scars ran from his right shoulder to his elbow. He rotated his shoulder, and the scars burned in protest as the skin pulled tighter than it should. The memories of the horrific car accident tried to push their way to the front of his mind. Parker had

3

gone two nights without the nightmares that had plagued him for the last year. They hadn't been peaceful nights, dreaming he was lost in a giant building and searching for the escape that didn't seem to exist, but it'd been progress. So much for the hope he was finally moving past them.

The sounds of the jaws of life cutting him out of the car still reverberated through his skull. He shuddered, goosebumps peppering his skin. The nightmares were bad enough, but the lingering sensations after he woke were nearly as acute.

His beagle, Happy, jumped onto the bed. With a warm tongue, he licked Parker's arm as though he were trying to wash away his owner's foul mood. Good old Happy. The only one around him who hadn't treated him differently since the night that changed his life in more ways than one.

With a deep inhale, Parker pushed the memories — and the effects of the nightmare — into the dark recesses of his mind. Where they ought to stay.

He hugged Happy and gave him a hearty pat before getting out of bed. Parker's first goal was to put the silicone-based gel on his scars. His doctor wanted him to consider laser surgery to reduce the depth of them. More time in any kind of medical setting didn't appeal to him. He'd rather wear long-sleeved shirts to cover them up.

He forced his attention on his to-do list for the day. This was the start of his second week back in his hometown of Kitner, Texas. After years of avoiding his family's ranch, waking up in his old room was still surreal. Mom had insisted he take it easy when he first moved in again, but if he had to be here, he'd earn his keep. They had five longhorn cattle coming in this afternoon, and he needed to oversee the process. Of all the goings-on at the ranch, the longhorns were the animals Parker dreaded working with the most.

He couldn't believe there was a time when he enjoyed everything about the ranch and working cattle. Especially the longhorns — Dad's personal project. But that was before his dad died of a heart attack when Parker was seventeen. After that, everything reminded him of Dad, and the loss burrowed into his chest with every ranch-related task he took on.

The ranch had been a success long before his dad passed and, in the midst of her grief, his mom struggled to keep up with it all. She'd hired people to manage the different daily needs of the ranch. Parker never blamed her for that — she did what she had to do. But it was never the same without Dad. Mom was never the same.

Parker had been the face of the family business since he was old enough to stand in a pair of cowboy boots and hold a lasso. A photogenic child, his parents had used him in promotions about their award-winning Angus cattle. Later, success on the rodeo circuit had meant high-paying endorsement opportunities.

He'd had a successful career. More than successful — he couldn't go anywhere without women recognizing him from the magazines and advertisements or men bringing up the products he endorsed. Until the accident put a quick end to that, too. Who wanted images of a man with a marred appearance on the cover of their publication? Losing the endorsements had been bad enough. But the damage to his arm had put an end to his rodeo career as well.

He'd struggled to make a living for nearly a year

before admitting defeat. Having to stay and work at home again only added insult to injury. He'd never tell his mom or sister that, though. God help them, they thought they were making things easier. It'd break their hearts if they knew the whole arrangement only made him feel even more like a failure.

The temptation to hide out in his room for the morning was strong. He wasn't ready to face the flood of memories that the longhorns were sure to bring forth. But he and Happy had an appointment at the hospital first thing, and there were children looking forward to their visit. His trip there every Monday morning was one of the few things that brought relief to Parker's daunting week. He'd focus on that and then deal with work when he returned. It was time to cowboy up.

He hoped he could get out of the house without running into anyone. The nightmare had left him grumpy, and he knew he wouldn't be good company.

Voices reached him the moment he got downstairs. He paused before entering the sitting room, faced with the image of his little sister as she twirled in her wedding dress. He still thought of her as a kid. When did Kara get old enough to date, much less become engaged? He had to remind himself that she was twenty-three. At five years his junior, she was certainly old enough to move on and create a family of her own. She was happy and her fiancé, Ben, was a stand-up guy. Goodness knows he put up with a lot when it came to their family.

Their mom, Gwen, was fiercely protective of her little girl and Ben was the first guy to make it through her intense scrutiny. That alone earned Ben a large measure of respect as far as Parker was concerned. He knew they were going to be happy together.

Mom held her hands clasped in front of her as she observed Kara. "You look amazing, honey. I can't wait to see Ben's face when he spots you coming down that aisle." Moisture gathered in her pale blue eyes.

Kara rolled her own eyes. It might be a sign of frustration, but her expression proved she loved the mothering. At least most of it. The two had always been close, leaning on each other after Dad died. Their connection had made it easier for Parker to pull away from the family business as soon as he could.

"Mom. Please. It's still almost a month away." But her objections became muffled as arms went around her, pulling her in for an embrace.

Parker hid a grin behind his hand. Most people knew Mom to be a shrewd business woman, and they would be right. But she was also one of the most sentimental people he'd ever known. He had no doubt she'd be crying at the wedding. Boy, he was glad he wasn't the first of the two of them to get married.

"You're my baby. I'm not sure I'll ever get used to the idea of you moving away. I'm not ready for my little girl to get married." Mom cleared her throat, blinked tears away, and turned. She spotted Parker in the doorway. "Isn't she beautiful?"

"Yeah, she is." That was the truth. She'd had boys following her around from the time she turned eight. After Dad died, Parker stepped in as her protector. He'd had to threaten more than a handful of them to treat his sister with respect. He didn't think Mom knew about most of them, and that was probably for the best.

Mom nodded her satisfaction and fixed Parker with one of her no-nonsense stares. "Did you find a date for the wedding yet?"

He suppressed a sigh — something that took a great deal of effort. This was one of the myriad of reasons why he'd hoped to sneak out before being noticed. He wasn't up to this conversation, especially this early in the morning. Why Mom felt like he needed a date to his own sister's wedding was beyond him. But Kara wanted one of those big, fancy weddings, and Mom was thrilled with the decision. She was determined that everything would be perfect and apparently, the brother of the bride attending solo shattered a wedding rule that no one had bothered telling him about.

Parker was certain, if he ever got married, he'd have a nice backyard ceremony with family and close friends only. No insane rules and regulations. No press. Just a quiet event where he could focus on his bride.

Would Mom be disappointed? Probably. Not that it mattered. Parker never pictured himself the marrying type before his accident. It certainly wasn't on the radar now. He swallowed down his frustrations.

"No, I haven't found a date. I was hoping you'd change your mind about that." He didn't have a girlfriend. Not a surprise with the road maps gouged into the side of his face and arm. Any woman who gave him a second look only did so to study the valleys in his skin. Then she'd act embarrassed once she realized he'd caught her staring. It was as if women had no idea what to do with him or how to talk to him. Because, of course, having scars on his face meant he spoke in a different language now. But he hated the head shakes of pity the most. He'd take disgust or embarrassment any day.

There was no way Mom would let this one go. She smoothed some of the fabric on Kara's dress. "One of my friends has a daughter your age. I'll call tomorrow and see if she's free."

"Absolutely not." The insistence in his voice brought a surprised expression to her face. "I'll either find a date on my own, or I'll go alone. But I do not want you setting me up with some random, unmarried woman."

Mom didn't appear convinced but said nothing.

Kara shot him a look of sympathy. Her face pouty, she mouthed, "I'm sorry."

Good grief. The last thing he wanted to do was cause trouble for her wedding. He gave her a wink, hoping to set her at ease.

When both women were convinced the dress still fit perfectly, Mom left the room.

As soon as she was out of earshot, Kara turned to Parker. "I hate that she bugs you all the time. I figured, with me getting married, she'd ease up a little."

"One would think." But that was Mom. She'd been like that since he'd turned twenty. In the eight years since, he'd had to deal with her trying to set him up with several girls. She'd stopped pressuring him for a few months after his accident. But now, she was pouring it on as strongly as ever, saying he needed to get back to normal. That it would help. Yeah, he doubted that. Especially when normal no longer existed.

Kara laid a hand on his shoulder. "You don't have to bring a date. You know it doesn't matter to me."

He knew she meant that and appreciated it. He pulled his little sister into a hug. "Thanks. But I want your day to be perfect — free from negative comments no matter who they're directed toward." He stepped back and held his arms out. "I'll find a date. Myself."

Kara's smile warmed him. He'd do anything for her.

"Thanks, Parker. I'm glad you're home again. I love you."

"I love you, too. Now I'm getting out of here before I get sucked into any wedding preparations."

Parker kissed her cheek and found his mom to kiss her on the way out.

"Don't forget about the longhorns coming in," she reminded him.

He fought to keep the bitterness simmering inside from boiling over into his voice. Just because he dreaded having anything to do with the longhorns didn't mean he had to cue anyone else in on it. "I won't. I'll be there."

Since coming back home, he'd agreed to take over organizing everything at the barn. From feeding schedules, breeding programs, and coordinating the different people hired on at the ranch, it was more than a full-time job. Parker did a lot of the repairs himself as well and that's what he focused on his first week back. Mom frequently reminded him it wasn't in his job description. Parker didn't care. He usually took Happy with him, and the two of them were more than content to work with no one else to bother them.

But all of that would wait. First, he needed to stop and grab a cup of coffee at the Stripes on his way into town, then it was off to the hospital. He'd take bringing a moment of happiness to a child over anything in his own life right now.

~

Chelsea Blake adjusted the Bluetooth piece in her left ear. "Seriously, Laurie. What was I thinking? I should've said no. Can you see me working on a farm?"

There was no mistaking her older sister's poor attempt to cover a laugh. "No. Not in a million years. But this is a ranch. Tuck said the family's been around for generations. They hired you as their coordinator. It's not like you'll get there, and they'll have you mucking out the stalls."

"You'd better be right." Chelsea rolled her eyes. She might have petted a horse twice in her life — and that was being generous. Or was it a pony? What was the difference, anyway? She had no desire to ride one, much less clean up after a whole barn full of them. Imagining the piles of manure was enough to cause her nose to wrinkle.

The Wilson Ranch was fifteen miles outside of town. She'd never even noticed it before, so it must be off the main highway. Right now, fifteen miles felt like an eternity.

"You'll do fine." Muffled crunching accompanied the assurance.

Chelsea chuckled, imagining Laurie sitting with a bowl of food balanced on her large belly. At thirty-two weeks into her pregnancy, Laurie was always eating something. "I sure hope so. I've got to make this work."

"You are putting way too much pressure on yourself, Chels. You need to do what's best for you."

"Sure. But Mom and Dad will be here in less than three weeks. I need to have a full-time job by then." Thinking about their parents visiting from whatever country they were currently touring filled Chelsea with trepidation.

Laurie sighed. "I'm proud of you and how far you've come. They will be, too."

Chelsea didn't believe it for a minute. And she knew Laurie didn't, either. Their parents had a fit when Laurie chose to leave their wealthy lifestyle and pursue a career as a photographer. As the sibling left behind when Laurie moved away, it wasn't pretty. She got to hear all kinds of things about how they were disappointed in their oldest daughter and how Laurie was setting herself up to fail.

They'd frequently talked about how at least one of their daughters still had the good sense to stay in New York and do what was best for her and the family. That's exactly what Chelsea thought she was doing at the time, too.

Her whole future had been lined up for her. Until she realized it was Daddy's future instead.

She'd left it all behind and if their parents were unhappy before, her decision made them livid. It'd been over a year, and the sisters heard all about it over Christmas. Their parents visiting Kitner this month meant another opportunity to berate their daughters in person.

Except that Laurie was happily married, expecting the first grandbaby, and had a stable job.

Where was Chelsea? Living above her sister's photography studio and working for a temp agency. Oh yeah, she'd set up all kinds of targets for them to aim their cannons at.

"You still there, Chelsea?"

"Yeah. I'm here."

"Hang in there. You'll do great. Call me this evening and tell me how it went."

"I will. I'm going to stop and use the bathroom before I get out of town. That's the last thing I need to do when I arrive at the ranch. 'Hello, Mrs. Wilson.

Before we get started, can I go pee real quick?' Nope, that's not happening." Just thinking about it sent another round of butterflies careening madly in her stomach. Laurie chuckled on the other end of the line. "Sure, you go ahead and get a good laugh at my expense." Chelsea giggled along with her and shook her head. "Hey, I'd better get going. Thanks again, Laurie. I'll talk to you tonight. Have a good day and don't work too hard."

"I'll try not to. Good luck, girl."

The connection went silent, and Chelsea concentrated on her directions. The town of Kitner faded behind her as a red and white sign for a gas station appeared in the distance. Not her first choice of bathrooms, but it might very well be her last before she drove into the middle of nowhere.

After parking, she headed inside to use the facilities and then browsed the drink selection. She was surprised to find the flavored iced teas she usually picked up at one of the health food stores in town. She hadn't even known such a thing existed until she'd moved to Kitner and Laurie introduced her to them. When she lived in New York, she'd never thought to try blueberry iced tea. Now she was addicted to the stuff, and Laurie happily took credit for bringing her over to the dark side.

Chelsea paid for the tea and a bag of chips and headed for the door. Once outside, she tucked the bottle under her arm to fish her keys out of her pocket. Someone was walking her way, so she sidestepped to make more room.

Something pressed against the back of her knee and she yelped. The glass bottle slipped from her arm to shatter at her feet, blueberry tea splashing her shoes.

*No! Not today!* She whirled to find a beagle staring up at her with curious brown eyes, its tail wagging, and tea dripping down its legs. Chelsea's gaze followed the leash clipped to its collar across the pavement and back up to a large, tanned hand clutching the other end. She finally focused on his face. A series of large, white scars ran from his hairline on the right side to an inch below his jawline. She took in his hazel eyes and hair that reminded her of brown sugar. Self-conscious, she lowered her gaze to the pavement.

# Chapter Two

Happy had started sniffing the woman's leg before Parker could pull him back. Now tea was all over Happy and they were expected at the hospital in a half hour. The woman was looking down at her shoes. Had she cut herself on some of the broken glass? "Are you okay?"

She slowly lifted her face until her gaze intersected with his. He took in her green eyes, dark blonde hair, full face, and red lips. His pulse sped up and his mind sorted through a list of phrases he used to use when he first met a beautiful woman. One was on the tip of his tongue, and that's when her attention became riveted on his scars.

His stomach fell into his shoes as reality settled in. They would always be what someone else saw first. Nothing else about him seemed to matter. She dropped her gaze so she was no longer staring, but the damage was already done.

"You should watch where you're going." He pierced her with a glare of annoyance. "Now I'll have to clean him up, and we have somewhere to be."

The woman's brows rose. "Excuse me? You should keep your dog on a tighter leash." She blew some hair out of her eyes and groaned. With a glance at her feet, she used her hand to brush at the darker spots of fabric where the tea had splattered on her black dress pants. It was barely visible.

Happy finished licking the tea off his paws and moved toward the puddle on the sidewalk, but Parker tugged him back. "You'll get cut up, Happy. You know better than that." He released an audible sigh. "I guess I'll clean up this glass before anyone steps on it and gets hurt."

She dried her hands off on her pants and then visibly shivered as a cold breeze blew through. "Don't bother. I wouldn't want to inconvenience you, or your dog," she said with an air of exasperation. Before she could kneel to clean up the glass, Parker tied Happy's leash to the bench and picked the shards up himself. Within seconds, he was depositing them into a trash bin. He pulled the cuffs of his black, long-sleeved shirt down and retrieved the leash.

The woman crossed her arms in front of her. "Thank you for that."

He shrugged. "Don't you need another bottle of frou-frou tea?"

An array of emotions played across her face before she gave him a tight smile. "I'm good." She tossed hair over her shoulder, ducked into the cab of her car, and shut the door.

Parker watched as she drove away. He probably shouldn't have said what he did. But it was the truth, wasn't it? If she'd been more careful, she wouldn't have run into his dog.

Happy tugged on his leash as though he wanted to

tail her. Parker held firm. "Come on, boy. You know better than to follow a pretty face."

His words surprised him. He'd been nothing but annoyed the moment she'd stared at his scars. At the same time, what he said was true. It was impossible not to acknowledge her beauty.

But she was like every other woman he met. She'd stared at the scars on his face until he caught her doing so, then kept her gaze averted.

So what? She'd avoided looking at his face. He couldn't blame her. He didn't like seeing it in the mirror himself. What was it about the jagged lines on his face that made people tiptoe around him as if he were some kind of monster?

Parker thought about how he'd acted around the woman. He hadn't exactly given evidence to the contrary. He should've apologized for Happy bumping into her, picked up the glass, and moved on.

The familiar tendrils of doubt and self-consciousness wound around his heart and drove him to his SUV. There were kids at the hospital waiting for Happy to come and cheer them up. That's who he would focus on now.

Pushing thoughts of the woman aside, he drove to the hospital and then guided Happy through the halls to the pediatric ward.

Parker and Happy had barely entered the area when two kids in the hallway saw them. Wide grins appeared as they ran toward them. Both kids went to their knees on the floor, and Happy was more than ready to cover them with doggy kisses.

Nurse Kay walked up and slipped her hands into the pockets of her brightly colored scrubs. "They love it when you two come to visit. Norman woke up asking

17

about you."

Parker smiled at the smallest boy patting Happy. With that joy on his face, you wouldn't know Norman had been at the hospital for three weeks now. Parker didn't know the specifics of his illness, but he'd seen the discouraged expressions on his parents' faces and knew it was serious. It was a privilege to be part of something that brought joy to the boy's day.

There was a community room in the pediatric wing where kids played video games, worked on puzzles, and visited with each other. Parker and Happy migrated that direction, gathering more children along the way. By the time they got to the room, there were eight kids vying for Happy's attention.

Parker sat on the floor with them, showing them how much Happy liked to have his ears rubbed. Then he pulled a soft ball out of his pocket and let them take turns throwing it so the dog could bring it back to them.

A little girl with olive-colored skin, dark eyes, and black hair cut to make her look like a pixie raised her hand. She didn't wait for Parker to say anything before voicing her question. "What happened to your face?"

The first few times kids asked him that question, it'd thrown Parker. But not anymore. "I was in a car accident a little over a year ago. I got hurt and had to stay in the hospital for a while just like you. But I got better and you will, too." He gave her a good-natured poke in the belly, and she giggled.

He fielded questions about Happy and his injuries with ease. That's what he liked about kids. They asked honest questions and then went on with life. Not like the adults who were afraid to ask what had happened, but either stared or acted uncomfortable. He'd prefer it if they questioned him and then moved forward with their conversations.

His thoughts shifted to the woman he met at the convenience store. What went through her mind when she saw his face? Was she repulsed? Curious? It didn't matter because he likely would never see her again, which was probably just as well. If her expression as she slammed her car door closed was any sign, she might deck him if she had the chance. The thought brought a grin to his face. She had a lot of spunk. It was something he'd always found attractive in a woman, and it wasn't a trait he ran into often.

Half an hour later, several of the children looked tired. Parker knew it was time to take their leave. The kids groaned in disappointment as nurses took their hands and led them to their rooms where they could rest.

Nurse Kay intercepted him at the elevator. "Thanks for coming, Parker. It always does a world of good for the kids. Same time next week?"

"We'll be here."

She waved and headed back to the ward.

Parker led Happy out of the hospital. Nothing squeezed Parker's heart like the view of children in the hospital. They should be out running and playing, not tied to wires and monitors. It didn't matter whether they were dealing with a temporary illness or if it was a lifelong battle, they always had a positivity about them. He wished he could understand how to harness it for himself.

Finding time to visit had been easy when he wasn't employed. Now that he was working at the ranch again, he'd have to juggle his time. Yet another thing he wasn't looking forward to doing. Parker unlocked the door of his SUV waiting in the parking lot. Happy claimed the passenger seat, and they headed out of town.

He didn't like relying on his family for a place to live. But at least he could hide out there and maintain a level of privacy.

Ironic how, a few years ago, he jumped at opportunities to be in the public eye. Being a successful team roper had opened more avenues than he'd ever thought possible.

Now, all he wanted to do was remain invisible. If he could accomplish that, he'd avoid run-ins like he'd had with the pretty girl at Stripes.

~

Chelsea worked to even her breathing and get her frustration under control. Who did that guy back there think he was, anyway? If he'd kept that dog under control, none of this would've happened. Now she prayed she could find her way to the Wilson Ranch without getting lost because she had little time to spare.

She tried to push the man and his dog from her mind but instead, replayed the scene over and over again. Even with the significant scars, he was incredibly handsome. She tried to imagine how he might appear if he cracked a smile.

And what had she done? Stared at him like he was Quasimodo or something.

Chelsea would've smacked her forehead against the steering wheel if she weren't driving. Heat climbed her neck. Thank goodness she'd never see the guy again.

According to the GPS on her phone, the ranch should be right around.... There.

It was game time.

As she approached the Wilson Ranch, which seemed a lot more like a mansion, Chelsea was reminded of her parents' home in New York. She'd grown up there and felt every bit a part of the lifestyle that surrounded wealth. But now…

She'd changed, and she wasn't keen on returning to this kind of environment. It was too late now. She was already here and wasn't about to disappear on the first day of work.

But as she entered the front door, she saw this place was as different as night was from day when compared to the home she grew up in. Her childhood home had been lavishly decorated and not remotely homey.

This was like a large-scale cabin. The floors were gorgeous hardwood shined to the point she imagined you could slide across them in stocking feet. All the furniture was a distressed white wood that fit the décor on the walls perfectly. Even the plush furniture was pretty, yet somewhat simple in design.

Chelsea kept silent as she followed the woman who opened the door to a sitting room of sorts.

"You can wait here for Mrs. Wilson. She should arrive momentarily."

"Thank you." Chelsea cleared her throat, waited for the other woman to leave, and then sat gingerly on the couch. It faced a tall, brick fireplace with flames dancing as it warmed the expansive space. She welcomed the heat, grateful to be rid of the chill she'd gotten outside. *Okay, God. Please help me to stay calm and not make a fool of myself.*

Chelsea didn't know what she expected from Mrs. Wilson, but the woman who entered appeared far younger than she would have guessed. Everything about the way she moved reminded Chelsea of her grandmother. But she didn't look like she could be over fifty.

She should have done more research on the ranch before coming here. Rising to her feet as Mrs. Wilson came closer, Chelsea tried to shove down her ever-growing nerves. "I'm Chelsea Blake, ma'am."

"Yes, I've been expecting you. You can call me Mrs. Wilson. I'm not a big fan of ma'am." She smiled, wrinkles at the corners of her eyes deepening. She seemed to size up Chelsea.

Thank goodness she'd chosen to dress nicely. Laurie had teased her, suggesting she should wear jeans and spurs. Not on her life. "I appreciate the opportunity to work for you. Pam at the agency has briefed me on the job requirements, but I'm looking forward to learning more."

Chelsea swallowed hard as Mrs. Wilson raised an eyebrow and nodded slowly.

She thought this initial meeting would be a short one followed by some kind of training. But when someone brought in a tea service — complete with several choices of pastry — she got the feeling they'd be there for a while. The next two hours were spent discussing Mrs. Wilson's expectations regarding Chelsea's job. By the time they finished, it was clear the job would entail a lot more than she originally thought it would. Somehow, she pictured sitting at a desk in an office, managing paperwork, and answering the phone all day. She might do some of that, but it sounded like she would also be an assistant of sorts to her new boss.

Mrs. Wilson asked her to hold on a moment and picked up her phone, speaking into it. "I've hired someone to work as coordinator, and she begins today.

Yes, I understand that, but it'll take a lot of pressure off you. I've gone over the preliminary details. I'd like for you to come and escort her to the barn, show her the office, and answer any questions she might have." A pause. "Yes. Okay, we'll be in the sitting room." She hung up. "My son will be here to show you around. He manages our hired hands and the livestock. You'll be working with him, and he'll be the one you should speak with if you have any questions. He'll refer you to me if it's something he can't help with." She sipped tea from her dainty china cup.

Chelsea reached for her own but didn't take a drink. She'd be working in the barn? Near animals? That was not in the job description. Surely they didn't expect her to have anything to do with them.

"Pam mentioned this job is temporary, but that you may hire permanently. Is that still the case?"

Mrs. Wilson nodded. "It is. I want to make sure whoever we hire permanently is the right person for the position."

That was fair. Which meant she had to do everything she could to prove to them she could do the job well.

The sound of a door opening broke through her thoughts. Footsteps echoed down the hall and into the sitting room, closely followed by a tall man in boots.

Chelsea gasped and jumped to her feet. There was no forgetting the scars on his face or those expressive hazel eyes. He was the man from the gas station.

Naturally she'd be working for him. The way the morning had gone, she shouldn't have expected anything less.

Stifling a groan, she set her cup down again and focused on Mrs. Wilson.

"This is my son, Parker. Parker, this is our new employee, Chelsea Blake."

Parker leveled her with an incredulous stare before taking long strides forward to stand directly in front of her. "Ms. Blake." He held a hand out to her as he clenched his jaw.

Chelsea's eyes were glued to the path of the scars. She shook his hand, which was significantly warmer than hers, and he released it almost immediately. She was staring again and jerked her gaze to her hands clasped in front of her, willing the pink to stay out of her cheeks. *I've got to stop doing that!*

"I'll let Parker take it from here. You'll find there's parking back by the barn, if you'd be so kind to use that from now on. If you have any questions, please ask Parker."

"I understand. Thank you, Mrs. Wilson. I appreciate this opportunity."

Mrs. Wilson smiled kindly and turned to leave the room.

Great. Now she was stuck with Mister Grumpy Guy, who clearly was as shocked to see her as she was him. This could be a never-ending day. Assuming Parker didn't fire her on the spot.

"If you'll follow me." Parker escorted her through the house and to the front door again. "I'll meet you over there." With a tilt of his head, he turned and walked away.

Chelsea's chest tightened as one worry chased another in her mind. First thing's first: She had to find her way to the barn and hope she didn't get lost along the way.

~

Parker had argued with his mom several times about hiring someone to take over coordinating everything on the ranch. He had it covered and, quite frankly, didn't want one more person to deal with. He should've known Mom would disregard that and hire someone anyway. He'd only been back from visiting the kids at the hospital twenty minutes when he got the call from her to come and show the new employee around. When he walked into the room, the last person he expected to see was the woman with the frou-frou tea from the gas station.

He wasn't sure if he was more annoyed or amused. What were the odds? Judging by the look on her face, she wasn't at all happy to run into him. He caught her examining the side of his face again. Yeah, they were obvious. But some hint of decorum would be nice. You don't stare at someone's injuries, no matter how hideous they might be. He was glad he was wearing a long-sleeved shirt. At least she couldn't ogle the scars on his arms, too.

With any luck, she'd get lost trying to find the barn and decide the job wasn't worth it to her. Meanwhile, it'd give him the time he needed to gain some semblance of control over his emotions.

He dealt with many people that judged him by the scars. Why did this woman doing the same irk him so much more?

It took Chelsea almost fifteen minutes to pull up in front of the barn. By then, he was leaning against the outside wall, waiting for her.

She was wearing the same clothes she had on at the convenience store. The black dress pants had somehow made it through the drive without a crease in them. Her blouse — some black and white floral print — fit her perfectly, hugging and flowing in all the right places. Black dress shoes finished the outfit. And every aspect of it was completely inappropriate for working at a ranch, though he was certain it had impressed Mom.

Chelsea's dark blonde hair was loose, flowing to the middle of her back. Strands along the side curled slightly and blew in the wind as she walked. She'd brought a heavy jacket with her and she pulled it on, holding it together in front of her.

She was a beautiful woman. In his old life, he'd have flirted with her, complimenting her on how her green eyes reminded him of fresh grass after a summer rain. He wasn't that man anymore. He straightened, ready to take anything she dished out. It was the flash of something akin to worry that stopped him. Maybe she wasn't as self-assured as she came off. Good. That should make it easier to get her to quit.

They stared at each other as if it were some kind of showdown. Parker shoved his hands into his pockets. "It took twenty minutes to wash the tea off my dog's feet."

Chelsea sighed, momentarily closing her eyes. "I'm sorry. This is my first day at work, so getting my shoes wet was an inconvenience for me, too." She lifted one foot and held it out toward him. A few dried drops of tea were barely visible. "It wasn't like I set out to ruin your day."

"It's too late for that," he mumbled under his breath. A slight exaggeration, but still.

"Excuse me?" She raised an eyebrow and planted her hands on her hips.

"Enough of that. There's work to do."

Her eyes narrowed, and he wasn't sure she believed his change of phrase. Finally, she waved at her car behind her. "Is where I parked okay?"

"Yes, that'll be fine." He nodded toward her shoes. "It can get a little muddy around here. I suggest more common-sense footwear from now on."

"I didn't think I'd be interacting with the livestock at all." Her green eyes grew wide and she swallowed hard.

*Was she nervous around animals? Perfect.* "We all pitch in and help where needed. While working with the livestock may not be your primary job, you need to be prepared." He enjoyed watching her squirm a little.

She kicked gently at a rock and nodded. "Okay." Her head turned to take in the longhorns grazing in the field in the distance, and she shifted her weight as though she were nervous.

She peered up at the red barn behind him. He could understand her awe. Dad had spared no expense when he designed the place. Photos of it were included in the Kitner annual Christmas cards pack that the city's information center sold every year.

"Let me show you around. Please remember that you're to have nothing to do with the animals unless specifically asked."

"No problem."

Was that relief on her face? He stepped to the side and motioned for her to go inside before him. It took a moment for his eyes to adjust. "Here on the ground floor are the stables for our horses. We have five of them. The stock room is here and the field closest to the barn is our small herd of Texas longhorns. We have another barn on the other side of the property dedicated to the Angus cattle we raise for beef."

Remembering how much Dad loved those longhorns was painful. There was no way he could avoid them and he'd seen them multiple times since he'd moved back home. But he had gotten no closer to them than the barn. Couldn't make himself. There were too many memories. He refused to go into too many details for Chelsea and led the way to the staircase that ushered them upstairs.

Parker had an office up here though he didn't use it, preferring to take his laptop to his room. He opened the door to the other space dedicated to maintaining the ranch activities. Normally, it might have been dusty for the lack of use. But he knew well enough that Mom would have made sure it was cleaned and waiting.

He was right. The light illuminated a spacious room with a desk, laptop, small fridge, microwave, and a set of windows that looked out over the pasture behind the barn. "This is your office. You're welcome to take the laptop home if you need to, but please remember that it belongs to the ranch. We'd prefer that you not install games or any other personal programs on it."

"Do I look like a gamer to you?" The moment the words were out, she pressed her lips together. Her cheeks turned pink as if she couldn't believe she'd spoken the words aloud.

Parker stopped and studied her face. She blushed easily. The combination of color in her cheeks and those big, green eyes… His pulse picked up tempo.

"No, you don't." Parker tried to imagine what she did for fun, but he squashed the thoughts almost immediately. It didn't matter what she enjoyed doing. She wouldn't last long enough here at the ranch for him to find out. With her back straight as a rod and those shoulders squared, he doubted she could appear more serious. "I hope you're familiar with keeping track of contacts, using Excel and Word, and accessing a database." He already knew the answer to that question. Mom wouldn't have hired her if she wasn't.

"I am."

"Good. Set your stuff down, and I'll show you how we have everything organized."

For the next hour, he showed her the database of all the employees, explained how the daily schedule worked, and went through the duties they expected her to fulfill. Even as he talked, his mind was going over different situations that might help convince her to quit her job. The sooner he didn't have to deal with her, the better.

He was close enough to her that a section of her hair brushed his cheek. He took a quick step back to put space between him and the soft tendrils. "It's half past eleven. You get an hour for lunch. If you need more than the fridge or the microwave, let us know."

Chelsea's green eyes bore right into him. "This will be fine."

"Good. We have a shipment of cattle coming in this afternoon. The company knows to come by here first so someone can sign off on them. I'll meet you here and show you how that works. Be ready at two o'clock sharp."

"Understood."

He suppressed a grin. If she lasted longer than two days working at the ranch, he'd be shocked. He had to check and make sure preparations had been finished for the new delivery. But mostly, he needed to escape the room that now smelled like a mixture of sunshine and honeysuckle.

# Chapter Three

Chelsea closed her eyes, willing herself to stay in control. She refused to let the disgust she was experiencing show. It wasn't directed at the cattle being unloaded into the pen or any of the men working with them. It was entirely because of the mud she was standing in. There was nowhere to go where the ground wasn't mushy after all the rain that had pelted the area the day before. She shifted her position; the mud coming up over the edges of her dress shoes to squish between her toes. The pantyhose may as well not be there for all the good it was doing. A shudder traveled up her spine. All she wanted right now was a long, hot bath. And she wouldn't say no to some chocolate. At least the temperature had warmed into the high fifties, so there was that.

She forced her attention on the activity in the pen as some of the ranch hands managed the cattle. She'd expected Parker to direct from the sidelines. Instead, he'd gotten right into the pen, oblivious to the mud splattering random designs halfway up his boots. He dodged the horns of one of the cows and directed it into the pen. His biceps bulged beneath the long-sleeved shirt he wore. He was clearly no stranger to hard work. Somehow, that surprised her.

When she'd run into him at the convenience store, she pictured him as one of those guys who bummed around all day nursing a beer. But here, watching him work, he seemed to know what he was doing. How often did the son of a wealthy woman like Mrs. Wilson work his own ranch?

If her parents had owned a place like this, you could bet they'd hire enough people so they didn't have to step a toenail in the mud. The thought of her mother standing where Chelsea was now lifted the corners of her mouth. Mom wouldn't have been caught dead out here, and if she had, Dad probably would've had to carry her back out again.

She tried to remind herself that some people paid good money to soak their feet in mud. She was getting that for free. Nope, it didn't help.

She caught Parker observing her, his eyes narrowing. What was he thinking about? Was he upset about the spilled tea this morning? Annoyed that she was working there at all? It was probably a toss-up.

Chelsea averted her gaze and focused on one particular cow that refused to cooperate. It tossed its head back and forth, shying away from a ranch hand. Its long horns hit the metal railing with a loud thunk.

Chelsea had seen longhorns before, driving past ranches on her way to somewhere else. She knew they were large animals. But being there, a short distance from them, it was clear how powerful they really were. A new respect for the cattle — and the men working them — grew. That respect almost included Parker.

Almost.

Parker turned and caught her eyes again. With an expert sidestep to avoid the horns and a firm shove of his arms, he directed the last reluctant cow through the gate before striding toward Chelsea. "That's the last one. It's a particularly good lot." Pride tinged his voice, but there was something else in his eyes. Sadness? Uncertainty? It was gone as fast as it had appeared.

"Are all five males?" Chelsea almost hadn't voiced the question. But if she was going to be working here, she wanted to know what she was talking about.

He paused as if he expected her to retract the question. "These are all females. Yearling heifers. We brought them in as an addition to our breeding stock."

"I didn't realize they had horns, too. I thought only males had them."

"No. You're thinking antlers, like you see in deer and elk. In cattle, males and females both have horns. In some breeds, the horns are removed at a young age, especially from heifers. We don't do that here with the longhorns." His eyes traveled over the new additions to the herd. "Texan longhorns wouldn't be the same without their horns."

Chelsea had to agree with him there. Whether she liked animals or not, these were magnificent to watch. From a distance. "And why are they called yearling heifers?"

The additional question seemed to catch him off guard. He blinked at her. "It's actually somewhat complicated. When a female is born, she's called a heifer calf and then, at a year old, she's considered a yearling heifer. After having her first calf, she's called a first time heifer. After her second calf, she's considered a cow from that point on."

"Seriously?" That was unnecessary. Call them all cows. Everyone knows what a cow is. "Is it just as convoluted for the males?"

"Almost. When he's born, he's considered a bull calf. Once he's a year old, he's a bull. If the bull is castrated, he becomes a steer."

Chelsea winced when he said the word "castrate". But who could blame her? Considering Parker was a man, he should've winced himself.

"Since you've never worked a ranch before, I don't want you out here with the animals unless someone else is with you." His voice had almost been normal when he answered her questions before. Now it was gruff again, as though it annoyed him to be standing here with her at all.

"Yeah, you don't have to worry about that." The cattle quieted down and were busy checking out the hay that had been forked into the pen. Other questions came to mind. Chelsea considered waiting and looking them up online. Maybe if she showed interest, he wouldn't think as badly of her. It was worth a shot, especially if it helped her keep the job. "So, will most of the cows bred here be eaten?"

"We raise Angus for beef and that's what makes up the majority of the stock. We only have thirty head of longhorn. Well, thirty-five now. We process some of them, but most are bred, and the calves sold to other ranchers across the United States or for use on the rodeo circuit." He shifted his weight, resting one of his muddy cowboy boots on the lower rung of the pen. He took his leather gloves off and let his arm lay against his raised knee. "We have several award-winning bloodlines and a waiting list a mile long for the offspring that result."

If there was such a long list, she could imagine people must pay a pretty penny to purchase them. And if the longhorns were only more of a side business, it was no wonder the ranch was so successful.

His gaze traveled down to her feet. "You know the practical footwear I recommended? I suggest you seriously consider those for tomorrow." Chelsea glared at him. His frown remained in place, but a small sparkle lit up his hazel eyes. "Come on, I'll drive you to the barn. There's no way you're walking back in those." He turned and led the way to the pickup truck he'd used to drive them down there earlier.

She glanced at her feet. Her shoes used to be black. She doubted they'd ever be the same again. A squishing noise made her grimace when she lifted one foot and then the other. The barn could be seen from where they were now. But the thought of walking there with all the slime between her toes.... She shuddered. Pretending she couldn't feel the mud shifting around under her feet, she hurried after Parker.

During the ride back to the barn, she wasn't sure what bothered her more: That Parker basically said, "I told you so," regarding her shoes this morning, or that he'd insinuated she'd be walking around in the mud again tomorrow.

She studied him from the corner of her eye. Or maybe what bothered her the most was the fact that, except for the mud, she'd enjoyed seeing Parker manage the cattle. Watching him work just might make coming back tomorrow a little easier.

~

"It's not funny."

"Oh, yes, it is." Laurie snorted and slapped a hand over her mouth.

Her husband, Tuck, laughed even harder after that, leaning his dining room chair back and shaking his head.

Chelsea wanted to throw something at her sister. She'd just told them about how Parker insisted she go and watch the new cattle being unloaded into their pen. She curled her toes at the memory of how the mud had surrounded them. She'd tried to clean her feet when she got back to her new office, but it made little difference. The rest of the afternoon, her feet itched thanks to the dry mud.

Thankfully, she hadn't run into Mrs. Wilson again. And she'd already decided which shoes to wear tomorrow. Especially if Parker intended to drag her outside for other goings-on at the ranch.

Laurie brought her laughter under control and feigned a look of sympathy. "I'm sorry you had to go through that. It sounds like he's about as fond of you as you are of him."

Chelsea set her fork down and huffed. "He wasn't happy to see me, that's for sure. He has horrible scars down one side of his face. The way he acts, you'd think I put them there myself."

Tuck appeared thoughtful. "He was in a bad car accident a year or so ago. I wasn't on duty at the police department that day, but I heard they had to cut him out of the car. If I recall correctly, he was in the hospital for several weeks. He was lucky to be alive at all, and it ended his career on the rodeo circuit."

Chelsea sat up straight. "You know him? Why didn't you warn me the guy was a serious grump?" And he was a rodeo cowboy? She tried to picture him riding a bull or bucking bronco, but couldn't quite conjure up the image.

"I don't know him. Only what I've heard from other people and read in the local newspaper." Tuck shrugged.

A twinge of regret twisted in Chelsea's gut. So he'd had a rough time. It's not like she'd been the one to cause his accident. She tried to imagine being trapped in her car like that and shuddered.

Tuck jabbed his fork into the air. "The guy was a media magnet and local hero most of his life until he dropped off the radar after his accident."

As far as the man's personality went, Chelsea had a hard time seeing him as someone the media would focus on. But looks? Take away the scars and oh, yeah. A handsome cowboy like that was sure to have quite the female following. She made a mental note to search for some background on her new employer later. If nothing else, she'd better understand where he was coming from. Or at least have some ammo to return fire. She took a bite of her salad.

"You'll be fine, Chels. Give it some time."

Chelsea nodded at Laurie's words. She had almost three weeks to get comfortable in this new job before their parents came to town. Even better, if she could convince them to make her position permanent, then it'd be one less thing her parents could criticize her for.

Mud or no mud, the Wilson Ranch and that brooding cowboy would not get the best of Chelsea Blake. She needed to stay on Parker's good side and show him she could do her job well. She thought back on how Parker had handled the cattle expertly and the way his hazel eyes had held her own.

Working at a ranch of any kind may be way outside

her comfort zone, but Parker had better watch out because this city girl didn't scare easily.

~

Parker lifted his racquet as Ray served the ball. They'd been playing for nearly an hour, and Parker was worn out. The friends used to play racquetball often, but it'd been way too long. His muscles agreed with the assessment, and his arm ached from his injury. They'd decided this was the last point of the game and when Ray bested him, Parker happily admitted defeat.

"You are out of shape, my friend." Ray downed half a bottle of water.

"I have a ranch to run now. I get plenty of exercise, just a different kind." Parker was used to Ray's jabs. And the truth was, he exercised nowhere near as much as he had before his accident. In fact, back then, he was about as much of a jock as Ray still was.

Memories of the many evenings Parker joined the guys for games of basketball flooded his mind. They had a team in the league and Parker was as competitive as any of the others. It was one of the few things he had participated in that was outside the rodeo circuit.

Ray had tried to get him back into the game many times over the last year but Parker refused. He hadn't wanted to see the pity on the faces of his buddies so he'd shut them out. Ray was the last of his friends he spoke to regularly.

He'd be lying if he said he didn't miss it all: the rodeo, the roping, playing basketball. Everything.

Ray polished off the rest of his bottle of water and pointed a finger at Parker. "You know, anytime you're ready, you can come back. The guys still ask about you sometimes. And we have a lot of new players."

"Not going to happen."

"It's been a year, man. Zeke's engaged and getting married in April. Cory and his wife just had their second child. And Julio's got a steady girlfriend." At that last point, he raised his eyebrows for emphasis.

Parker bit back a sigh. His old friends had moved on with their lives. And where was he? In the same place he'd been a year ago. He always enjoyed seeing Ray. They'd been best friends for years. But he could do without the attempts to draw him back into his old life, especially one he felt little connection to anymore.

It was time to change the subject. "How's Jessie?"

"She's good!" Ray's entire face changed as he talked about his wife of two years. "We found out she's pregnant last week."

"Wow, that's great!" When Parker first met his friend, he'd never imagined he'd get married, much less become a father. Apparently time did change a man. "Congratulations. I'll bet you're both ecstatic."

"We're over the moon. They weren't kidding when they say pregnant women glow."

Parker listened as Ray talked about how they planned to tell their families tonight at dinner.

Knowing how excited his mom was for Kara to get married, he could imagine how thrilled she'd be when the first grandbaby was finally on the way.

He pushed down the sadness that sometimes made its way into his heart when he wasn't prepared. He'd never considered himself the marrying type. Then he met Brenda. But after that didn't work out...

Kara insisted there was a woman out there who would look past his scars and see him for who he really was. But it was hard for him to imagine.

No. He doubted marriage or children were in the cards for him. And he had to be fine with that.

Ray must have asked him a question because he was staring, waiting for a response.

Parker shook himself from his reverie. "What's that?"

"Earth to Parker. Boy, you are out of shape. I was asking if you had a woman in your life right now."

"No. Not a one." And it was better that way.

The friends said goodbye and Parker got into his SUV.

An image of Chelsea crashed into his mind out of nowhere. She'd been watching the longhorns and hadn't noticed his observations. The combination of her smile with the way the breeze blew her hair around her face... He swallowed hard.

It really hadn't been necessary for her to come out when they unloaded the new longhorns. But he'd hoped that getting out there in the mud would deter her from coming back. He knew those fancy shoes of hers wouldn't last long.

He pictured her lifting those mud-laden shoes, pure disgust on her face, and laughed loudly. That almost made up for having to deal with her at all today. Another day or two of similar outings, and hopefully she'd be calling it quits.

Her questions about the longhorns had thrown him, though. It was clear she wasn't real comfortable around the animals. But where he had expected disinterest or even boredom, she'd responded with curiosity.

He needed to up his game a little. Because if he had any say in it at all, little Miss Frou-Frou would be gone by the end of the week.

# Chapter Four

Chelsea spent half the night with her good friend Google, searching for information about the Wilson Ranch, and Parker in particular. She'd hoped to find a tidbit or two and found pages of news articles. The ranch was bigger and more successful than she'd originally comprehended. And Parker? He'd been in the limelight for ages and that was no exaggeration.

Apparently, he'd roped as a young child. Chelsea found a variety of pictures showing him in team roping competitions, and many of them earned him first place. Her research led her to discovering that wins and his popularity landed him two big endorsements.

She did another search and found a picture of him in jeans, no shirt, with a coiled rope resting over his shoulder. Chelsea let out a low whistle. With that knock-down grin, the guy was a regular heart throb. No wonder one of the largest names in Western wear had snatched him up as their advertisement eye candy.

Curious about team roping, she located a few videos of Parker's competitions online. The announcer stated

Parker was the heeler and his partner, Trace, the header.

A steer was released from a pen and both Parker and Trace raced their horses after it. Trace swung the lasso over his head and roped the steer around both horns. His horse pulled back, turning the steer to the left. Meanwhile, Parker kept his own lasso swirling above his head, roping the steer's two rear legs, sending the animal to the ground. The entire thing took under eight seconds.

Chelsea watched several videos, amazed at the coordination required by the duo to rope the steer in an amount of time that put them on the top of the boards.

Even though she should get to bed before having to get up early for work tomorrow, she kept browsing pictures from Parker's past. Images of him with a woman on each arm had shown up more than once. By all online appearances, the man had been given everything he could possibly want.

And then there were the pictures of the car accident. Chelsea flinched the moment one of them appeared on the screen. How had anyone survived that giant pile of jagged metal that used to be a vehicle? She tried to imagine what it would've been like to be trapped inside, but she couldn't. It only left her claustrophobic and willing away the inklings of pity she felt for the man.

Other news articles reported that his injuries had destroyed any chance of returning to the circuit. Chelsea surmised it would've been impossible to walk away from that kind of accident without it altering a person.

She'd like to hope he'd been pleasant to be around before. All of those images she'd seen in the news, from the time he was two until a year ago, told of a confident man who had a funny story to tell. It sure didn't match up with what she knew of her current employer and made her more than a little curious about him.

~

The next day, Chelsea drove right past the main house to park near the barn like she had done after that first meeting. She killed the engine and took in a deep breath.

"The courageous Chelsea Blake enters day two in the wild Texan outback," she said to herself in her best Australian accent, following it up with an eye roll. The sun had shone all day yesterday and hopefully some of that mud had dried up. If she were lucky, she wouldn't have to go outside at all. But if she did, she was prepared.

She got out of the car, a tote bag in one hand, and her usual bag over her other shoulder.

There was no sign of Parker, which was just as well.

She made her way into the barn and up to her office. The lights were still off. She switched those on, got the laptop running, and put her lunch in the fridge.

A list of things that needed to be done was by the computer. Chelsea had no way of knowing if it was Mrs. Wilson's handwriting or Parker's. But it was relatively straight-forward, and she got right to work.

After a couple hours of silence, footsteps echoed from the stairs. She looked up as Parker peeked his head around the door.

"I see a little mud didn't keep you from coming back."

Was he happy about that or disappointed? Chelsea studied his face and had no clue. He ought to play poker — he'd sweep the table. She raised an eyebrow. "I don't quit easily."

"You got my note. Any problems with it?"

Ah, so it was Parker's handwriting. Exceptionally neat and flowing — that detail surprised her. "None at all. I should be finished in an hour."

He checked his watch. "Very well. Meet me downstairs at two." With that, he disappeared from the doorway.

Chelsea stared at the space he'd left behind, half expecting him to return and elaborate a little. He never did. She tried to speculate on what horrible outing he had planned but then worked to get everything finished up. Before doing anything else, she traded her slip-on shoes for the boots she'd bought the evening before. They weren't what she would have worn normally, but they came up nearly to her knees and would be a lot more practical than the shoes she wore yesterday.

She intended to be downstairs early, but he was already waiting for her in the truck.

"Hop on in." There was no missing his scrutiny as he checked out her footwear once she'd climbed inside. "Those are an improvement. Not pretty. But an improvement."

She lifted one of her boots and rested it on the dashboard. "Are you kidding? What's wrong with them?"

"Are they cowgirl boots or rain boots?"

Chelsea studied them and finally shrugged.

"Exactly."

With a huff, she let her foot fall back down to the

floorboard. Well, they were more appropriate, just like he'd asked. If he'd wanted her to wear a uniform, he should have specified. She could've sworn she heard a chuckle, but when she swung her head in his direction, his face was a stoic as ever.

Chelsea let out a slow breath of air. "Where are we going?"

"Bringing new cattle in requires more than relocating them. Depending on where we get them from, they have to be quarantined for as long as a month or two. This lot was purchased from a place we trust, so we'll integrate them into the rest of the herd in a few days. Meanwhile, we've brought in a vet to give each of the yearlings a once-over. Our vet is here regularly, and I thought you should be introduced. That way you're familiar with who he is."

Okay. Well, this shouldn't be too bad. She rested her arm next to the window as the landscape bumped by. With all the money the family made, you'd think they could pave more of these dirt roads.

When they got to the pen, she noticed a large diesel truck and trailer waiting. Parker got out of the truck and before Chelsea had the chance to, he'd opened her door for her. She slipped to the ground, and said, "Thank you," under her breath. A gentleman. Who would've thought?

He said nothing but led her around the side of the pen. A large, metal contraption held a yearling. An older man was just outside with his hand on the animal's back. The moment he identified Parker, he stuck a hand out and gave a big grin. "Good to see you, Parker. You've got a nice looking bunch here."

Parker shook the man's hand and nodded. "One of the best I've seen in a while." He motioned Chelsea forward. "Mom hired someone to coordinate everything here at the ranch. This is Chelsea Blake. Chelsea, this is Doctor Rick Emerson. He's been working with us for a long time."

Doctor Emerson tipped his hat at Chelsea, and she waved her greeting. "It's nice to meet you."

"You, too, young lady. Yes, I've been here for a while. Worked with this guy's daddy many years ago." He shook his head and sadness passed over his face momentarily. "He was a good man, may he rest in peace."

Parker cleared his throat, and Chelsea thought he appeared uncomfortable. She'd read that his dad had died when Parker was seventeen. What kind of relationship did they have? She hoped they'd been closer than she was with her own father. Other than conversations around the dinner table, she could count on one hand the number of instances she'd spent quality time with him. Not that it was a lot better with her mother.

She frowned and tried to shake the thoughts from her head. She motioned to the device the veterinarian was standing outside of. "What is this?" It reminded her of a security station she'd walk through at the airport only a lot more elaborate. She walked around the front to where the yearling's head was.

Parker grabbed her elbow to stop her. "Stay back here away from her horns." When she'd retreated to his location, he let go of her arm. "This is called a chute. It's designed to allow the animal inside and keep it contained. There's not enough room for her to kick or move those horns of hers around. It keeps us — and her — safe. Meanwhile, she's secure and the doctor here can examine her, administer vaccinations, and do anything else that needs to be done to ensure her health."

It looked claustrophobic to Chelsea. The yearling shifted her weight and twisted her head to one side. She couldn't go far, though, thanks to the bars of the chute keeping her horns trapped. "What do you check for?"

Doctor Emerson gave the animal he'd been examining a hearty pat on the rump. "Longhorns are especially healthy animals. So thankfully, they don't get sick often. I'm making sure their vaccinations are up to date and then, since this particular lot will be incorporated into the breeding program here, we're branding them." He nodded to another man on the other side of the chute.

If Chelsea had known what would happen next, she might have averted her eyes. But without warning, the hot brand was pressed against the yearling's skin. With a grunt, the animal shifted away from the electric brand and into the side of the chute. Chelsea jumped back, relieved the chute held firm.

Parker reached out and scratched the yearling's head as though she were a large dog. "Sorry about that, girl," he said, his voice barely above a whisper. The walls holding her in place were loosened and the gate in front of her opened. She walked out, trotting across the pen to join two other yearlings that must have already gone through the check-up process.

The scent of burned hair and flesh reached Chelsea's nostrils and she wrinkled her nose. That combined with the smell of manure didn't exactly inspire thoughts of dinner. The animals were amazing to watch, though.

"They're surprisingly graceful for their size."

Parker turned to face her, his gaze unfocused. "Yes. They are magnificent." His voice sounded sad. He rubbed a hand across his chest and stepped away.

Chelsea hoped that, by asking questions, she was showing Parker she wanted to learn about the animals and was dedicated to her job.

They spent the rest of the workday watching. How often would she be invited to go on these excursions? Chelsea looked down at her new boots. Mud marred the sides of them and she gave a little shrug. At least it wasn't squishing between her toes this time. Being outside was actually pleasant. And it was almost lonely in the barn by herself. The morning had positively dragged and being out here was a lot more interesting. She snuck a quick peek at Parker. As much as she hated to admit it, the company could be a lot worse.

Besides, the guy liked dogs and had a way with longhorns. How bad could he be?

~

Satisfied with the clean bill of health Doctor Emerson gave the new additions to the herd, Parker smiled. He shook the good doctor's hand and thanked him for his work then watched the truck and trailer disappear from sight.

Dad would've been happy with this lot. He'd spent most of his free time out here with the longhorns. Parker had vowed he'd grow up to run a ranch dedicated to longhorns. He'd been so sure of those plans as a boy. Until Dad died.

Unwilling to allow the melancholy to take root, he turned to speak with Chelsea and found she'd moved off to the other end of the pen on the opposite side of the cattle. She stood on the lower rung of the railing, her elbows hooked over the top. The breeze caught her hair and whipped it around behind her. Sunshine brought out golden highlights and with the longhorns in the background, the combination was stunning.

Her first day at work had been a joke. It was clear she'd never stepped foot on a farm of any kind. Add in those ridiculous shoes and he'd had a good laugh at her expense when she wasn't looking. But now...

She'd exchanged her dress pants for a pair of whitewashed denim jeans. The sweater she wore was nice, but practical. And those boots. If a pair of galoshes and a pair of cowgirl boots had offspring, he imagined what she wore would look exactly like that. They were terrible. But they were more practical than the footwear she'd sported the day before. There was something about it all that struck him.

She was cute.

He sobered. So what if she was cute? She still didn't belong on a ranch. As soon as he'd laid eyes on her, he'd acknowledged she had a pretty face. But Mom was normally picky about who she hired. Chelsea had no experience on a ranch. Where had Mom found her? What on earth had inspired Chelsea to take this job? Was it because she'd be working for a high-profile employer? Was she hoping to get her foot in the door and work her way up to where she was getting a larger piece of the Wilson Ranch money? The questions swirled around in his mind.

Yesterday, he was certain if he got her out and showed her the messy side of ranching, she might decide this wasn't the job for her. And if she quit, maybe Mom would let things be. But Chelsea dealt with it far better than he'd thought she would. And right now — boots aside — she appeared to belong there.

That was dangerous on so many levels.

Parker strode toward Chelsea. As he got closer, her expression stopped him. He'd expected to see disgust. Or exhaustion. The interest and contentment surprised him. It seemed like, just when he thought he had a good handle on the type of woman Chelsea was, she'd go and change things up.

He stepped up onto the bottom rung beside her.

Three of the yearlings chased each other at the far end of the enclosure. Chelsea laughed. Another breeze blew through, carrying with it the scents of sunshine and honeysuckle he was coming to associate with her. Was it her shampoo or a perfume? He fought to keep his eyes on the herd and not get another peek at her.

"I never knew cattle could run so fast. Calves, yes. But not adults."

Parker scratched the back of his neck. "They can surprise you. You should see the whole herd run. Not as graceful as a herd of horses, but still amazing."

"I'll bet." Her voice was wistful.

"Have you ever ridden a horse?"

"Never." She used her fingers to rake the hair away from her face.

Parker sensed hesitation in that one word. "Don't tell me you're afraid of them."

She refused to look at him and shrugged. "I'm not afraid." She squared her shoulders and Parker wasn't convinced. "I'm not good with animals. I haven't been around many of them."

Parker couldn't imagine not having animals. "You

didn't have a dog or cat growing up?"

Chelsea barked a humorless laugh. "My sister and I begged for a puppy for years. Our parents said they were too dirty."

Now that was sad. She might be good at the computer-aspect of this job, but a respect for the animals and at least a limited knowledge of them were nearly as important. He checked his watch. "It's after five. Time for you to get out of here. I've got fences that need mending."

He stepped away from the pen and toward the pickup truck. He heard her scramble to catch up with him, her large boots clomping against the ground. It was a fight to keep his face neutral.

Several of the ranch hands had stopped what they were doing to admire her. Obviously, Parker wasn't the only one who found her pretty. Which meant there was even one more reason to hope she quit her job. None of them could afford the distraction.

Well, if she didn't seem to mind the outdoor work, maybe it was time he switched gears.

Parker dropped her off at the barn with a nod of farewell and went back to the house. Poor Happy had been cooped up off and on through most of the day. Now that Parker was finally heading out to make repairs, he could bring Happy with him. Some mindless, physical work was exactly what he needed to get his new employee out of his head.

# Chapter Five

Chelsea was bored out of her ever-loving mind. She slowly let her head tip backwards until it rested against the top of her chair. When Parker had first dragged her outside on Monday, she thought this would be the worst job she'd ever had. Well, aside from her short stint at a perfume store where the fumes had about done her in. But she'd dressed differently, bought new footwear, and she thought things went well on Tuesday. Aside from insinuating her boots were odd looking, Parker hadn't criticized her choice of attire, and he answered her questions about the longhorns. She'd gone home that night and didn't hesitate to put a mark in the win column.

In fact, when she got to work Wednesday morning, she'd anticipated going out and checking on the new members of the herd.

Except she'd arrived at work to find a dozen boxes waiting for her in her office. She'd barely had time to count how many there were before Parker appeared.

"Good morning. I see you've found the boxes.

We've had these in storage for years. These are the bills of sale, some land records, and other invoices from the eighties that never were computerized. I'd like for you to scan them in so we have digital copies of it all."

Chelsea's jaw dropped. "You're kidding."

"No, ma'am." Parker hefted one box and set it on her desk. He pulled a handful of files out. "Let me show you where you'll want to save these." He then took the next thirty minutes to walk her through the steps and their filing system.

There was nothing complicated about it. But five boxes... Chelsea seriously doubted she could get through them by the end of the week. The end of the month, maybe. She bit back a sigh. Paperwork was necessary in any job, but she detested it.

Parker wished her a good day and took his leave. Chelsea stood glaring at the boxes, willing them to spontaneously combust. Five minutes later, they were still there, mocking her. Obviously, they would not scan themselves. She lowered herself into her chair with a groan.

All day, she kept hoping Parker would stop by and suggest an outing to check on the longhorns or something similar. She never did hear a peep from him. Thursday was a carbon copy of the day before. By the time Friday rolled around, she was going stir-crazy being stuck in the office.

Maybe the beginning of the week hadn't gone as well as she'd thought it had. Had she done something wrong? Was it silly she kept hoping Parker would appear and rescue her from this file-scanning prison? It didn't matter. She'd do the job he'd given her without complaint if that's what it took to be offered a permanent position.

By lunch, Chelsea decided she had to get out of there. She had an hour — and that was her time, which meant she could do whatever she wanted with it. And she was sick of eating there at the desk she sat at all day long.

Parker had warned her to stay far away from the animals. She wasn't about to go against that. But it didn't mean she couldn't watch them from a distance. The moment she stepped outside, it was as though a weight were lifted from her shoulders. Chelsea walked toward the longhorn pasture and found a tree that offered the perfect vantage point. She sat on the ground and zipped up her coat. She'd been warm enough walking but now the cold in the air permeated the layers of fabric. Still, it was worth it to get out of that office for a while.

Chelsea settled in and ate her lunch. The antics of the yearling heifers had her laughing several times. The trunk of the tree she was leaning against soaked up all the tension that'd been building in her neck and shoulders over the last couple of days. Yes, this was how she planned to spend her lunch hour every day from now on.

Her cell phone pinged, and she shifted to pull it out of her back pocket. It was a text from Laurie.

"Hey, sis! Tuck's working tonight. You want to come over for dinner? I'm making enchiladas."

Chelsea studied the remains of her sandwich and pictured the frozen meal she'd planned on eating that night. Her fingers flew over the keyboard. "Are you kidding? I'm there. I'll bring tea and chips. What time?"

"Six."

"Can't wait!"

She slid the phone back in her pocket. It would be the perfect end to a tumultuous week.

She'd finished the last bite of her sandwich when a sound pulled her attention toward the barn. A large horse clip-clopped its way in her direction with Parker sitting in the saddle on its back. It was the first time she'd seen the guy in two days. Where had he been?

"What are you doing out here?" he asked when he'd reached her location.

"Eating lunch. I had to get out of that office for a while."

He nodded slowly. "Making much progress on the old invoices?"

Chelsea could've sworn she detected a half smile, except that the sun shining down from above made it hard to see his face clearly. Well, she wouldn't let on she was completely bored to pieces.

"I am. I won't have it done for you this week, but hopefully they'll all be scanned in the next week or two." She hoped she appeared carefree.

He frowned and took in the field behind her. After a few moments, he brought his focus back to her. "Well, I'm doing a fence line check and could use some help if you have time this afternoon."

*You mean, not be stuck in the office the rest of the day? Yes, please.* "Sure. What can I do?"

"Get a notebook from the office and a pen. Keep track of the panels we need to either repair or replace. I can saddle up a second horse for you."

Panic gripped Chelsea's stomach, and she immediately shook her head. "I've never ridden a horse. That's not a good idea." She'd take the boxes of unending files any day.

"I thought you said you weren't scared of them."

~

Chelsea hesitated. She might have told Parker she wasn't scared of horses, but even the other day the truth had been written on her face. She'd probably never even touched a horse, much less ridden on one.

As much as he'd love to see her ride a horse for the first time, he wasn't about to put someone with no experience — and a big dose of fear — on one of their mares.

Apparently, the mountains of paperwork hadn't pushed her over the edge of quitting. The only thing left, as far as he was concerned, was pushing her past her comfort zone. And clearly, riding horses was way beyond that.

"Then you can ride with me." Okay, maybe that wasn't such a great idea. But her frown revealed she didn't like that option any more than the first one. And if this is what it took to get her to quit, he could handle the inconvenience. She'd certainly made it longer in his employment than he thought she would. It was time to make sure she didn't return next week. He wouldn't give her room to object. "I'll meet you outside the barn in ten minutes." With that, he tipped his chin and rode away.

Ten minutes later, she was waiting for him like he'd asked her to. When he stopped in front of her, she was gripping the notebook tightly enough to turn her knuckles white. He fought against the guilt that tried to push its way to the surface. "Hand me the notebook and pen until you get up here." She did as he asked and took a step back. "Eloise won't hurt you," he assured her. He certainly wasn't going to get the woman onto the horse's back if she wouldn't come within three feet of them.

Parker talked her through how to mount the horse and then held his hand down. She grasped it, and he pulled her up until she was sitting behind him. After handing the note-taking supplies to her again, he urged Eloise forward.

Chelsea gasped at the same moment her arms went around his waist as she tried to keep her balance. She tightened her hold until his ribs protested. Without thinking, he put a hand over one of hers. "Hey, I won't let you fall." What was he doing, comforting her like that? Didn't he want her to get frightened?

Yes, he did. Except that it was impossible to ignore the innate need to keep a member of the fairer sex safe. The idea of scaring her into quitting had been entertaining. But now that she was leaning into his back, hands trembling, he felt like a real jerk.

He kept Eloise's pace slow and steady, continuing to cover Chelsea's hand with his own. After a few minutes, she'd stopped trembling. "We're going to go around the property's fence line." It was something he'd been meaning to do, although it wasn't a high priority. "If we see anything that needs repairs, I'll tell you the locations and you can write them down."

He felt her nod against his back. "I don't know how anyone gets used to riding a horse."

Parker bit back a laugh. "It takes a while. I grew up on horses."

"I saw online that you used to rope."

He hadn't expected that to come up in conversation. He considered ignoring the comment. But she'd put so much trust in him by even getting on Eloise that he responded. "I did. My dad used to be a big name in team roping before he retired to focus on the ranch." He paused. "He took me to a lot of rodeos and taught me to rope steers at an early age."

"So you followed in his footsteps."

Parker shrugged. It was much more complicated than that. He had followed in Dad's footsteps in a lot of ways. But joining the rodeo circuit and all the advertisements he did for endorsements had been as much about escaping the ranch after Dad died than it was anything else.

He located a spot in one of the fence panels that needed to be tightened. Nothing that had to be addressed immediately, though. He told Chelsea what to write down, and they continued on their way.

Chelsea's hold around his waist had loosened, probably because she was getting used to Eloise's movements. Parker tried his best to ignore the feel of her arms but it was next to impossible. That, in conjunction with her warmth against his back and the scent of honeysuckle occasionally reaching his nose, and Chelsea was about all he could think of.

They were nearly through inspecting the fence when a leaning pole caught his attention. He was so relieved to have a reason to put some space between him and Chelsea that he brought Eloise up short. "I'll need to tighten this one before we head back to the barn." He helped Chelsea to the ground before getting down himself.

The moment she had her footing, he took in the way her messy hair softly framed her face. Her eyes sparkled, and she rotated her shoulders while rocking back on her heels. "I'm going to feel that tomorrow, I can tell already."

"Probably." Parker took two large steps back and turned toward the fence. "Riding takes a while to get used to."

"It wasn't nearly as bad as I thought. Eloise is a real sweetheart." Chelsea's voice was contemplative. Not at all as frightened or wary as he'd originally thought she'd be if he pushed the issue of riding a horse.

Parker put a hand on the leaning post and exhaled. Well, either Chelsea had a lot of nerve, or she was desperate to keep the job. Either way, it didn't appear he would get rid of her anytime soon.

What surprised him the most was the small dose of relief that somehow mixed itself in with the disappointment that his plans to get her to quit had failed.

~

Parker withdrew a tool from a leather case on his belt. He pulled the post straight and then tried to reach around it to tighten the wires.

"Can I help?" Parker grunted but didn't complain. She took that as a yes. Chelsea stood beside him and grasped the post, pulling in the same direction he was. A moment later, he had the wire tightened. They stepped back to examine their work.

"Much better," he said with a nod.

Chelsea battled with whether she should say

anything else about his past before curiosity won out. "Do you miss roping?"

His eyes widened as he raked his fingers through his hair. "Yeah, I miss it. But nothing to be done about it." He lifted his right arm. "Can't rope with a messed-up arm." He shrugged as if it didn't matter. "We'd better get back to the barn."

Chelsea moved away from the post but something caught the back of her shirt. She paused and turned her head, trying to see what was stopping her.

Parker noticed and stepped around her. "Hold on. Your shirt is snagged on a wire." He swept her hair out of the way and cleared his throat.

She prayed her face wouldn't flush as she felt his hands against her back. Her shirt was freed within moments. "Thank you."

"No problem." He didn't quite meet her eyes. He mounted Eloise and then helped her to do the same.

"I'm sorry if I overstepped with the questions. My brother-in-law mentioned you used to be involved in rodeos and I was curious."

She didn't think he was going to speak anymore until the barn came into sight.

"It was fun and intense. But it's not part of my life anymore."

He might make it sound like it was no big deal, but Chelsea could detect the regret in his voice. "I'm sorry."

Parker put a hand on hers for a moment before removing it. "It is what it is. Nothing to be sorry for."

~

Chelsea tried to focus on the paperwork the last hour of the day but wasn't having a lot of success. She kept thinking about Parker. When he had first suggested she ride Eloise, she'd thought her anxiety would lead to a panic attack. But something had happened the moment she put her arms around him and he'd touched her hand. She'd still been nervous, but his small attempt to reassure her had immersed her in a calmness she hadn't expected.

After a while, she found she enjoyed riding with him. She still couldn't imagine riding a horse on her own anytime soon, but the thought of it didn't elicit as much fear as it had before.

She could still feel the way his hand had covered hers. He was her employer and he barely tolerated her, but her heart still tried to pound its way from behind her ribs every time she thought about being close to him.

Spending time with her sister was exactly the distraction she needed. After work, she had enough time to get home, change clothes, and then swing by the store to grab the tea and chips before arriving at Tuck and Laurie's house.

She knocked on the door and heard her sister's faint, "Come in!"

The moment Chelsea opened the door, she was greeted by the couple's black and white border collie, Rogue. Chelsea set the bag down on the floor and crouched to give him a good petting. "You're a good boy. Are you hungry for some enchiladas, too?" It looked for all the world like Rogue bobbed his head. Chelsea laughed and locked the door behind her. She found Laurie working in the kitchen. "You shouldn't

60

leave the door unlocked like that. It could have been anyone knocking."

Laurie paused, a spatula in the air. "And if it hadn't been you or one of the core family members, Rogue would have told me so. That person wouldn't have a prayer of getting into the house." Rogue walked around the island in the middle of the kitchen to sit next to his owner's feet.

Chelsea moved to place the bottles of blueberry sweet tea and tortilla chips on the counter. "Don't you ever feed the poor guy?"

Rogue watched Laurie as she pulled a hot pan out of the oven. "You'd think not. He's been doing this all day. He follows me everywhere and as soon as I sit down, he's lying across my feet." She gently used one foot to slide him over a little. "I'd banish him to the backyard if it weren't so sweet."

Chelsea pulled open the bag of chips and crunched on one. Laurie wore an apron that used to fit her fine. But with that extended belly, the apron was much too small and looked comical. "You're going to way too much trouble. You know I'd have picked up dinner for you."

Laurie shook her head and placed a hand on her belly, rubbing it. "This little one would not settle for anything but enchiladas. Tuck made me promise to save some for him when he got home." She nodded toward the living room. "Let's eat in there. My back's bothering me and lounging on the couch sounds awesome."

They worked together to get the drinks and chips into the living room. Then Chelsea insisted that Laurie sit and put her feet up while she filled their plates and brought them out. Chelsea collapsed into an oversized chair, kicked her shoes off, and groaned.

"Rough day?"

"I rode a horse."

Laurie gaped at her. "You're kidding. And you survived?" She wrapped a string of cheese around the forkful of chicken enchiladas.

"Haha. Real funny." Chelsea licked a drop of red sauce off her knuckle. "I thought I'd finally made a good impression on Tuesday but apparently, I was wrong. I don't see him all week and then he insists I ride with him to check the fence line." She huffed and took another bite of her dinner. Yep, her sister definitely got the cooking genes in the family. "I don't get the guy at all. I never know if he's going to show me the ropes or give me the cold shoulder. It's driving me crazy."

"You mean you actually rode the same horse with Parker?" Laurie looked amused as she waggled her eyebrows.

"Way to stay on topic."

"I'm sorry, Chels. And I'm sorry the guy's so back and forth like that. As long as you have things to do, does it really matter?"

"Yes, it matters." Chelsea put her fork down on her plate. "I need this job. I've got to impress them all enough to be offered a permanent position."

"And your job is the only reason why you want to impress Parker?" Laurie tossed her a knowing look.

"He's not my type." Well, that wasn't entirely true. She'd always been a sucker for tall men with soft brown hair. Throw in those incredible eyes and he was totally her type. Sure, he'd acted the gentleman when it came to opening her door for her. And making her feel safe while riding Eloise. But otherwise, he'd been standoffish. "He's got issues. I have enough of my own to sink a small ship."

She noticed Laurie grimace and sat up straighter. "You okay?"

"I'm cramping a little tonight. I probably overdid it. Three clients may have been a little much."

"I'd say." Chelsea watched as Laurie rubbed her belly, inhaled slowly, and went back to her food. "You need to slow down. At least a little. Most women who aren't pregnant can't keep up with your pace."

Laurie shot her a look of annoyance.

They ate in comfortable silence until Laurie inhaled sharply and tensed. Chelsea stood up and took the plate from her, setting both of theirs on the coffee table. "You need to lie down."

That Laurie complied without argument didn't escape Chelsea's notice. It put her more on the alert. She checked the clock and noted the time. "Let me go get you a big glass of water. Make sure you get enough to drink. Close your eyes and take a nap. I'll clean the kitchen up."

Laurie nodded and her eyes slid shut.

Chelsea wasn't hungry anymore. She put up the leftovers, made sure Rogue had his dog food, and then kept an eye on Laurie. Several times during her twenty-minute nap, her face would change and her brows drew together as though she were in pain. She finally sat up and rested her head in her hands. A minute later, she scrunched forward and cradled her belly with both arms.

That was it. Chelsea jumped up. "You've been having cramps every five minutes or so. Laurie, I think we need to take you in and make sure you're not having contractions."

Laurie seemed like she wanted to argue. Instead, she nodded. "I need to call Tuck."

"We'll get you in the car first and then you can call him."

# Chapter Six

C helsea kept her eyes on the road ahead. Laurie
clutched her cell phone and held it to her ear as
she spoke.

"We're on our way. Chelsea's driving. Please, Tuck,
just meet us there." Laurie sucked in a breath. "I'm
nervous. It's too early."

It was all Chelsea could do to not watch as Laurie
hung up the phone and groaned with the beginning of
another contraction. Chelsea looked at the clock. They
were still five minutes apart but seemed to be getting
stronger. Not a good thing when Laurie was only
thirty-three weeks along.

A traffic light switched to red and Chelsea had to
brake behind a line of cars.

*Come on! Come on!*

The contraction must've eased because Laurie
released her grip on the arm of her seat. "I wish we
were in Tuck's car right now."

"Yeah, me, too." Tuck would turn the squad car
lights on and they'd be at the hospital in a fraction of

the time. Chelsea took the lull in forward movement to observe Laurie. "You okay?"

"I don't want to have this baby in a car."

"Yeah. I'm not fond of the idea, either." Chelsea had seen plenty of movies and prayed this was a case of Braxton Hicks contractions.

*Please, God. Get us to the hospital. Protect the baby.*

The car in front of her inched forward and then gained speed. Chelsea followed, going under the light as it turned red again. She released the breath of air she'd been holding. Barring any other issues, they'd be at the hospital in the next few minutes.

Tuck was waiting for them when they approached the entrance to the emergency room. Chelsea's car hadn't quite come to a complete stop when he pulled Laurie's door open.

"They've got a wheelchair coming for you." Tuck put one hand on Laurie's swollen abdomen. "You two will be okay."

Laurie nodded, her copper curls bouncing. She transferred from the car to the wheelchair when it arrived.

Tuck peered through the cabin of the car to Chelsea. "Thank you."

She nodded. "I'm going to park and then I'll be right there. I'll bring Laurie's bag with me."

Always the organized one, Laurie had her hospital bag packed a month ago. They'd all teased her about it and now Chelsea was glad. After finding a place to park, she retrieved it from the back seat and hurried across the parking lot, hoping to catch up with them. One lady in admissions told her they'd taken Laurie upstairs to labor and delivery.

Chelsea's stomach rolled, and she swallowed against the ache in the back of her throat as she rode the elevator up to the fourth floor. She stepped into Laurie's room. Seeing her sister lying on a hospital bed with Tuck standing over her gave her some relief. Surely the doctor could do something to stop the contractions now.

Chelsea set the bag down by one chair and went to stand at the foot of the bed. Laurie reached a hand out for her and Chelsea moved to hold it.

"Thank you for getting me here, Chels. I appreciate it."

"Anytime. Thank you for not putting me in a position where I had to deliver my own nephew."

Laurie laughed. A moment later, she closed her eyes against another contraction.

Tuck held his wife's hand, his eyes brimming with concern. Laurie knew he was skilled at handling anything his job as a police officer threw his way. She imagined being unable to help Laurie was driving him crazy.

A nurse came in along with the on-call doctor. "We're going to do an ultrasound and an exam to see where you're at."

That was Chelsea's cue. She leaned down to give Laurie a hug. "I'll be out in the waiting room."

Laurie nodded. "I'll send Tuck to get you in a few minutes."

Chelsea closed the door behind her and made her way to the waiting room, suddenly feeling lost. Sending silent prayers to heaven, she took a seat and withdrew her phone, only paying half attention to the game she turned on. She didn't want to contact anyone else. Not until Tuck and Laurie had more details about what was going on.

And hopefully there'd be nothing to share with the rest of the family except for a silly story about going to the hospital with Braxton Hicks contractions.

Giving up on her phone, she went to browsing through some old magazines until Tuck finally reappeared. His face was void of emotion, which put Chelsea on edge. She jumped to her feet.

Tuck pinched the back of his neck with one hand while using the other to escort her toward Laurie's room. "She's in early labor. Her cervix is dilated to one centimeter. They're going to start her on magnesium sulfate to see if they can get the contractions to stop."

"Okay. How's the baby?"

"He's doing fine. The heart rate is good. They'll give Laurie some steroids to help the baby's lungs just in case. Let's hope they won't be needed."

"I'll be praying that's the case." They reached Laurie's room, and Chelsea peeked inside. A nurse was skillfully inserting an IV. She taped the needle in place, set the drip on the bag of fluids, and left.

Laurie motioned them both closer. "She said it might take a few hours. But hopefully we'll see results quickly." She closed her green eyes and let her head rest against the pillow. Moments later, her eyes flew open. "I have a photo session tomorrow morning! Chelsea, can you call them and reschedule? Ugh, I feel horrible. The Davis family's been on the books for months."

Tuck took her free hand and gave her a firm look. "And with seven kids, they'll understand."

"I've got it covered." Chelsea took out her phone

and opened her note application. "Reschedule the Davis's. Check. What else can I help with?"

Tuck responded. "Go ahead and reschedule all of Laurie's clients for the rest of the weekend and next week, too."

Laurie looked like she might object. But when another contraction hit, its progress monitored by one of the machines, she nodded.

"Will do." Chelsea jotted a few more things down. She'd call and cancel, but didn't plan on rescheduling yet. Not until they knew whether the medication helped. She seriously doubted the doctors would send Laurie home to go back to her old routine. But Chelsea wasn't about to mention that now. "Is there anything else I can get for either of you?"

Tuck shook his head. "I'll call the family. Let them know what's going on."

Chelsea nodded. She sat in the chair next to the hospital bed and focused on Laurie as Tuck made the calls. It was after nine in the evening and there wasn't a thing she could do to help Laurie now but wait. It might be a long night.

~

Parker flipped through the Sunday morning newspaper until a photo caught his eye. He stopped and something twisted his heart.

*Brenda.*

His ex-girlfriend's face was the last thing he'd expected to see. The settee dipped when Kara sat beside him. She tapped the engagement photo of Brenda and a man named Walter, according to the text below it.

"You're better off without her. She was a gold digger." Kara's voice was steady but her face belied her emotion.

Parker wouldn't have believed it back then. But the moment his face had been marred, she'd ditched him without so much of as in-person apology. He'd since realized he didn't love her, but it still stung. Especially given the circumstances.

"Yeah, I suppose." He knew she spoke the truth.

Kara reached for the newspaper, wadded it up, and tossed it at the fireplace. She hit the bricks just to the right. It bounced off the floor and rolled under a chair.

She chuckled. "I was close. Don't waste too much time worrying about her. She's not worth it."

That was enough to coax a small smile out of Parker. It widened when his sister leaned into the corner of the settee and stretched her legs across Parker's knees. She'd been doing that since she was little.

"I'm surprised you're not with Mom going over more wedding plans."

Kara groaned. "Mom's busy with a meeting, thank goodness. I don't think I can take any more of it. If Ben and I could get married tomorrow, I'd totally do it." She sobered. "I'm glad you're walking me down the aisle."

"Me, too. Thanks for asking me." When she'd come to him wanting to know if he'd stand in for their dad, Parker agreed immediately. It'd meant more than he could express. "Dad would be proud of you. He'd have been all stoic during the ceremony and then probably cried like a baby later."

Kara blinked tears from her own eyes. "Sometimes I have a hard time seeing his face when I close my eyes now. Is that horrible? I had a dream last night that I'd forgotten him."

Parker understood. Many of his childhood memories had faded over time, and he was five years older than she had been when Dad passed. "Don't worry, you'll never forget him. Tell me about your favorite memory from when you were a kid."

"Bedtime. I remember saying my prayers and then he would pray over me, too. It was one of my favorite things." She let out a little sigh. "I still miss that." She paused. "Why don't we pray anymore, Parker?"

Parker had his own reasons for why he rarely prayed. Most of them in anger over his dad's death. Then he'd gotten out of the habit, completely consumed with his life on the rodeo circuit. Rarely did any thought of what God might have in mind for his life enter the equation. Then it was just reinforced by his accident. It was hard to believe God cared with all that had happened. At this point in his life, he was so used to leaving God out of his daily decisions, he wasn't sure how he'd even change that now.

But that wasn't the answer Kara needed. "Dad was the spiritual leader in our house. He was the one that prayed — before bed, at the dinner table. I guess, when he died, we missed that and no one wanted to take his place. Instead of carrying on like we should have, we let it go." The pain twisting in his gut told him it'd been the wrong thing to do. But at this point, opening back up in prayer seemed like such a foreign concept. Did God even want to talk to him anymore? "Do you pray, Kara?"

"On my own? Yeah." She shrugged.

"I never knew that."

"I guess I feel closer to Daddy when I do."

Parker knew he needed to lighten the mood. "Do you remember the tea parties?"

Kara's eyebrows drew together. "Vaguely."

Parker grinned. "When you were five or so, you loved tea parties. You'd carry your tiny glass tea set into the sitting room. You liked to draw invitations and give them to Dad, inviting him over for a party. Dad would sit on the floor with you and he'd have to use his fingertips to hold the handles of the cups. You'd pour water, clink your cups together, and sip tea while eating mini cookies on matching plates." The dreamy expression on Kara's face inspired Parker to continue. "One time, Dad had a hard time holding onto a teacup and it fell, shattering. You were devastated. He stayed up half the night piecing it together with super glue. When he gave it to you the next day, he said the cracks made it special. And you insisted on drinking from it every time after that."

A lone tear rolled down Kara's cheek and dripped onto her shirt. She swiped at it with her hand. "He was a good dad, wasn't he?"

"The best." Parker ran a finger across the bottom of Kara's foot. She jumped, curling her feet on the settee beneath her. "He'd want you to be happy on your wedding day. Remember that."

"Thanks." She leaned over and gave him a kiss on the cheek. "God's still there, you know." She raised an eyebrow. "I couldn't have made it this far without Him. I'll bet He misses you."

The doorbell rang and Kara launched herself off the couch. "That's Ben! He's picking me up for lunch." She hurried from the room to answer the door.

Parker followed, arriving just in time to witness Ben and Kara share a heated kiss. She blushed as they broke away. The men shook hands. "Good to see you, Ben. You sticking around for dinner tonight?"

Ben looked to Kara who nodded hopefully. "That'd be great. We should be back later this afternoon." He kissed the back of her hand. "I thought I'd treat my girl to a picnic in the park."

The way Kara was beaming, it was clear her fiancé's choice was a good one.

"You two have fun."

Kara waved as Ben escorted her to his car. Ben was a good guy, and Parker knew he'd do anything to make Kara happy.

He shut the door and sat back down in front of the fireplace. He laced his fingers together and leaned his head back into his hands. Kara's words replayed in his mind: *"God's still there, you know."*

Parker wasn't so sure about that. He'd felt alone after his accident. There were many times when he blamed God for the whole thing. But what if God had performed a miracle and saved him? If he was still on God's radar, why didn't He prevent the accident in the first place?

His thoughts flew through the events of the last few days. If it hadn't been for that accident, he wouldn't be back on the ranch now, the longhorns would still be a thing of the past, and he wouldn't even know who Chelsea Blake was.

Memories of how it felt to have her sitting behind

him, her arms circling his waist, flooded his mind. When he'd freed her blouse from the fence, he'd tried to ignore the way her hair had slid through his hand. He could still feel every single strand.

What was she doing now? She was probably on a date with her boyfriend or chatting with friends. He blew out a breath of frustration and stood from the settee. Whatever she was doing, it had to be a lot more exciting than anything he had to look forward to the rest of the day.

~

Chelsea closed her eyes against the bright lights in the hospital waiting room. It'd been a lengthy weekend. At first, the medication had worked and Laurie's contractions slowed. They'd even stopped for a while. Just when they were about to release her from the hospital to let her go home on bed rest, they started back up again. All attempts to stall labor failed after that.

It was one o'clock Monday morning and they were in the operating room, delivering the baby by C-section.

Poor Laurie was beside herself, upset that her plans for a medication-free birth had not only gone out the window, but had smashed to smithereens on the floor below. Tuck clearly felt helpless.

Much like the rest of the family.

Chelsea opened her eyes again and took in the surrounding people. Tuck's mom, Patty, sat across the aisle from Chelsea, her hands twisting over and over in her lap. Grams, Patty's mother, sat next to her. Unlike Patty, Grams seemed calm and collected.

Tuck's older sister, Lexi, worked as a nurse for a pediatrician in town and volunteered in the NICU there at the hospital. It was a big relief to all of them that she was being allowed to go into the operating room with the expectant parents.

Lance Davenport, Lexi's husband, continued pacing back and forth in front of the large window overlooking the parking structure below. "We should be hearing something soon."

"I hope so." Patty ran a hand over her eyes. "I can't believe this is happening."

Grams patted her hand. "It'll be okay. God's in control."

"I know, Mom. Praise Him that it isn't any earlier in the pregnancy." She wiped her hands on her pants. "Serenity texted and said she and Gideon will be driving down later today. She's got to talk to the staff and make sure she can get the time off."

Chelsea had heard nothing but good things about Gideon's special needs school where Serenity also worked. She was sure they'd understand the situation and hopefully they'd arrive before dinner.

Ugh. Work. There was no way Chelsea would call in sick or take the day off, either. Not after only one week at a new job. It would be a long day.

It was even more frustrating that she hadn't been able to get a hold of her parents to tell them about Laurie going into labor. You'd think, with a daughter in her third trimester, they'd make sure they were reachable. Apparently not. She'd left several messages on their phone and then given up. She'd be lying if resentment wasn't one of the many emotions she was toiling through at the moment.

Chelsea leaned forward, resting her elbows on her knees.

*Please, God. Please let Laurie and the baby be okay. Guide the minds and hands of the doctors and nurses. Be with Tuck and Laurie.*

She could only imagine how they were dealing with it all right now.

The next fifteen minutes passed as though they were going through slow motion. Patty was walking the aisle, Grams had doled out peppermints from her purse, and Lance was about to go ask for an update when Lexi came into the waiting area.

Chelsea stood, her stomach rolling. Lexi was smiling. It had to be a good sign, right?

Lexi's shoulder-length dark hair was still mostly hidden beneath a surgical hat. She slipped her hands into the pockets on the front of her purple scrubs. "Laurie's fine and the C-section was textbook. They're closing her up now, and then she'll be going to the recovery room."

"And the baby?" The question came from Patty.

"He's tiny. I wasn't going to tell you guys the weight and all but Tuck said I could. He wants to stay back there with him and Laurie right now. But he was born at five pounds five ounces and is sixteen inches long. A great size considering how early he is." She paused, and Chelsea sensed she was having to keep her emotions in check. "Laurie got to kiss him, but he was having a hard time breathing so they whisked him away to the NICU. I just came from there and we've got him stable, but he's on oxygen right now. We're going to start him off on C-PAP hoping we won't have to put him on a ventilator."

Lance ran a hand through his blond hair and released a lungful of air.

Chelsea knew how he was feeling. She'd hoped they would find out the baby was fine and there weren't any worries. But the truth of the matter was that there were likely going to be some complications.

Grams reached over and clasped Patty's hand.

"Things are going as well as we could have hoped for, guys. The baby's seven weeks early and often boys experience delayed lung development compared to girls." Lexi looked back at the door she'd come through. "I need to get back. Tuck asked if I'd stay with the baby so I'm going to go. Tuck or I will keep you guys updated, okay?"

Patty and Grams gave her a hug, and Lance kissed her briefly before she disappeared again.

Chelsea glanced at her phone. Still no call back from her parents. She chucked it onto the waiting room chair before flopping down on the one next to it.

Patty sat next to her and put a hand on her arm. "Honey, are you okay?"

"My parents should know about this. But I haven't heard back from them since I tried to get in contact with them on Friday. Isn't that messed up? I mean, is it just me?"

Patty put an arm around her and hugged her. "Who knows? Maybe their phone died? Or they've been in flight all this time to get here? International flights are a nightmare."

"Yeah, maybe." She doubted it, though. They'd always put their travels ahead of their daughters. Why would this be any different? "I wish I were back there to see for myself how Laurie's doing. I'm grateful they have Lexi."

Grams was still standing and she motioned everyone to her. "We have a new life to celebrate. A new member of the family. I have a great grandson who needs our prayers."

They joined hands and began to pray for Laurie, Tuck, and the baby.

Chelsea waited until they visited Laurie in her room and then caught a glimpse of the baby in the NICU. He was tiny, and with the C-PAP machine and the numerous wires and tubes around him, all they could see were his feet. Such teeny feet. Laurie was exhausted. Chelsea promised she'd come back the next evening.

She got home around three in the morning and hoped to catch a few hours of sleep before going to work.

After what felt like minutes, something pricked the edge of Chelsea's consciousness. She struggled out of her slumber, her eyelids like bricks. She was still in her clothes from the day before.

What time was it?

She blinked and tried to focus on the clock next to the bed.

8:30

*What?! No!*

She was supposed to be at the ranch thirty minutes ago. Why didn't her alarm go off? A glance at her phone told her she'd forgotten to plug it in before falling asleep. The battery had died. Fantastic, she couldn't even call Parker to tell him she was on the way in or explain why she was running late.

Parker wasn't going to be happy. And all this after

she felt like they'd made some serious progress on Friday.

She threw open her closet with a forceful groan and rummaged around for a change of clothes. All Chelsea could do was pray he'd understand and get to the ranch before her job had completely washed down the drain.

# Chapter Seven

Parker used the pitchfork to throw hay into the horse stalls with more force than necessary. With lips pressed together, he put every bit of his annoyance into the physical work. He noticed Happy was keeping his distance and he didn't blame him. He'd make it up to him later. Parker would take him out to the stock pond, Happy always enjoyed that.

For now, Parker was irritated he was on the ranch at all this morning. He should be at the hospital, talking to the kids. Instead, he'd had to reschedule at the last minute, pushing their regular visits to Monday evenings instead.

It shouldn't be a big deal. While the kids might have been disappointed, Nurse Kay assured him the change was fine and they'd all look forward to seeing Parker and Happy later that day.

But it was a big deal because Mom had pulled him aside Sunday evening. Now that Chelsea had joined the staff, Mom insisted she needed Parker on hand during the workday in case Chelsea had any questions. It irked

Parker to no end because he didn't think they'd needed to hire someone else to begin with. Besides, she'd been working at the ranch for a week now. She could manage for a few hours in the morning on her own.

Even as he fumed, he knew most of his reasons for being upset were selfish. Yes, he loved going to the hospital and talking with the kids. Watching their faces light up while they played with Happy made his week. But it was also his place to hide. A way to postpone the beginning of a new week where he had to interact with more people than he wanted to deal with. It was his buffer. Having that taken away made him as mad as anything else.

So yeah, it could've been worse. But it didn't mean he had to be happy about it.

*It isn't Chelsea's fault.*

The thought struck him out of nowhere. No, it wasn't her fault that Mom hired her behind his back. Or that Parker hadn't wanted to return to his life here on the ranch in the first place.

He sighed. After last week, he'd chosen to abandon his attempts to make her quit. She'd more than proven she could take anything he dished out. In fact, he was ready to tell her she didn't have to scan in the rest of the invoices since it really was just busywork to make her bored.

And while she had no clue what to do on a ranch, he couldn't deny she was trying her best. Spending time with her last week hadn't exactly been terrible, either.

Truthfully, he'd awakened this morning looking forward to seeing her. Until the time for her to show up for work came and went. He even walked up to the main house to see if she'd stopped there first for some reason. He finally pulled his phone out of his pocket. No missed calls.

Thirty minutes morphed into an hour late. Not exactly good etiquette for an employee, much less one as new as she was. His breath caught and his heart clenched. What if all his attempts to make her quit last week had worked after all?

This was why he shouldn't have let her get under his skin in the first place. Of course she'd leave, and why wouldn't she? He chucked the pitchfork into a corner and cracked his knuckles. Instead of finishing his work on the stalls, he walked outside, his body tense, just in time to watch Chelsea's car pull up.

She shoved the car door open and got out, pausing to duck back inside and retrieve her keys. Her hair, which was always well kept, looked like she'd just gotten back from a run outside. Her green eyes wide, words rushed from her like a horse shooting out of the starting gate.

"I'm sorry. I was going to call, but I forgot to plug my phone in. The time got away from me this morning. I…"

Parker held up a hand to stop her. All his frustrations with his mom combined with Chelsea being late and resulted in a volcano of anger. "You've been here a week. We rely on our employees to be on time unless you've arranged a day off or you're sick. Are you sick, Ms. Blake?"

"No, I'm not sick. But my…"

He didn't want to hear it. Mom owned this place, and he still had to be up every morning and was required to do his job. Chelsea was no exception.

"If you're late like this again without letting us know ahead of time, it will be your last day here. Do I make myself clear?"

Chelsea lifted her chin and squared her shoulders. "It won't happen again."

Parker whirled on his heel and beckoned her to follow him. "Before you go to your office and work on cataloguing the rest of the invoices, I want you to finish adding hay to the stalls." He picked up the pitchfork, scooped up some hay, and deposited it in the stall. "Three per stall." He motioned to the other side of the barn. There were still four stalls that needed hay.

Chelsea blinked at him as though she wasn't sure he was serious. "You want me to feed the horses?"

As a way of answering, Parker handed the pitchfork to her. He waved a hand at a stall.

Chelsea set her bags down, took the tool from him, and awkwardly scooped some hay. She dumped it over the fence.

"You're going to need to get more than that." She tried again, and Parker shook his head. He knew he was overreacting. But it was as if his mouth was going faster than his brain could process. It was a train wreck, and he couldn't have stopped it if he tried. "Again."

She did, struggling to lift more hay than she had before.

"You're doing it wrong."

Parker was reminded of the Chelsea he'd met at the convenience store, only this time she appeared ready to spit fire. She planted one hand on her hip and took two steps forward, the toes of her shoes touching his.

"You know what? This isn't in my job description."

She chucked the pitchfork to the ground and sidestepped away from it and him.

Anger erupted inside and Parker jabbed a thumb at her car. "Then quit. No one's stopping you. There's nothing keeping you here. If you believe I'm being unfair, then quit. If you think you can show up whenever you want to, you obviously don't need this job."

"You don't know a thing about me. I need this job more than you can imagine. If you want me gone, you'll have to fire me." She studied him, her brows knit together and the vein in her neck pulsing.

Her eyes followed his scars from the top to his neck. That only added fuel to the fire. "Go ahead." Parker turned his face allowing her to see them more easily. "Get a good look at them. They're all anyone sees."

Chelsea flinched but didn't back away. She crossed her arms in front of her. "You have quite the chip on your shoulder, Parker Wilson. And you want to know something? It's bigger than those scars on your face. I guarantee you people may notice the scars first, but it's your attitude and the way you treat people that make any kind of lasting impression."

With that, she swiveled on one foot, picked up her bags, and headed toward the stairs that led to the second floor. "I wish I knew what I've done to make you dislike me so much."

Chelsea's words hit Parker in the chest and they burrowed their way to his very core.

"I don't dislike you." But his words were pointless because she'd already gone and he'd barely spoken them above a whisper.

Everyone he'd known on the rodeo circuit had

treated him with kid gloves since his accident. He was sick and tired of people walking on eggshells around him. As though he might explode or fall apart if they told him anything remotely negative.

But Chelsea was different. Other than his mom and sister, and maybe Ray, she was the first person to stand up to him in a long time.

Part of him was annoyed beyond reason. Another part of him gained a lot of respect for her. Without warning, his body flooded with regret. He thought about Kara. What would he do if a man spoke to her the way he'd spoken with Chelsea? He'd deck the guy in a minute and make sure he was never that disrespectful to a woman again.

And if Dad were here right now, he'd have given Parker a right cross himself.

Parker would have deserved it.

"How'd I end up here, Happy?"

His dog walked tentatively from the other end of the barn, sad eyes trained on his master. He stopped and wagged his tail. Parker knelt to pat him. "Let's finish feeding the horses. I think this is a good day for some fence repairs."

Maybe the sound of a hammer hitting nails would drown the regret ricocheting around in his chest.

~

After leaving Parker downstairs in the barn, Chelsea went to her office, closed the door behind her, and seethed. How dare Parker have that kind of attitude toward her? How dare he try to punish her for arriving late by having her do work that she didn't know how to do, was outside of her job description, then criticize her for doing it wrong?

She walked back and forth between the door and her desk several times, fists clenched. She considered quitting and would have if she didn't need the job so badly. Especially now that Laurie's baby was here. Their parents may arrive sooner than they'd planned — assuming they ever bothered to check their phone and get Chelsea's message in the first place. They still hadn't called her back. She needed this job to turn into a full-time position. If that was even possible after having yelled at Parker just now.

She was stuck. Stuck at the stupid ranch. Stuck with Parker who apparently had a real issue with her. If he'd given her a chance to explain... Truth be told, she thought she'd made some progress with Parker. She'd hoped she was proving herself to him. Apparently, it'd all been in her head. That was probably what bothered her the most right now. She thought they'd gotten past their bad first meeting. Parker could hold a grudge. And if that were the case, there wasn't a blasted thing she could do about it.

For a while, she hoped he'd show up at her office. Expected him to come back and ream her again for being late or fire her on the spot. She wasn't good with comebacks in the moment, but she had several of them for him now. But he never did show.

She ate lunch while she worked to make up for the hour she was late. The anger she felt slowly evaporated, replaced with tears. With her teeth clenched and tears racing each other toward her jaw, Chelsea decided she wouldn't give Parker the satisfaction of quitting. She'd do her job — the one she was actually hired to do. And if he decided to fire her, he wouldn't be able to say it was because she'd slacked. She finished one box of invoices and left promptly at five. So far, it appeared she still had her job. How long would that last?

Now Chelsea sat in her car in the hospital parking lot, desperately trying to shake off her anger. Her emotions had oscillated all day, and she was exhausted. She took in a deep breath and tried to release her tension with the air in her lungs. Confident she could put aside her work issues for now, she got out of her car. The early evening wind was chilly as Chelsea walked purposefully across the hospital parking lot.

Warm air enveloped her as she entered the hospital. She consciously left the whole situation with Parker behind. She was here to visit her sister, and she wasn't about to let him mess that up, too.

Chelsea thought about the handful of texts she'd received as updates. They hadn't been much. It'd been torture having to work when she would've preferred to stay here at the hospital. She felt the weight of the bag of food she carried in one hand. She'd told Tuck she was bringing dinner. Right now, it was about all she could do.

Upstairs, Chelsea entered the waiting area to find Tuck's sister, Serenity, her son, Gideon, and Patty. "Hey, guys. How're they doing?"

Patty put some things in her purse. "They're doing well. Laurie's still tired, but she looks better tonight. We took Gideon to go see his new cousin in the NICU."

"That's great! What'd he think?" They were able to go up to the NICU and observe through the glass windows as often as they wanted. Chelsea prayed it wouldn't be too long before the sweet baby boy could be held by all the family that loved him.

Serenity laughed. "He'd been looking forward to it. But since you can't see much of the tiny guy, it was a little anti-climactic for him. It'll be different when he can reach out and hold the baby's hand."

"No doubt." Chelsea moved the bag of food from one hand to another. "I brought some contraband. There should be more than enough if you guys want something to eat, too."

Patty held up a hand. "Thanks, honey. But we're on our way out. You've got good timing. Laurie was just commenting about how she's finally hungry again."

Serenity nodded. "Gideon's done well, but we're about at his limit. We're going to stay the night with Mom and Grams and then head back home tomorrow. We'll be back this weekend. Aaron said he'd come with us."

"That'll be great." Aaron and Serenity had been dating for several months now and everyone in the family liked him. He was good for Serenity and did amazing with Gideon. It was no secret Patty hoped he'd ask Serenity to marry him soon. Chelsea had only met him twice, but he seemed like a nice guy.

"You go ahead and take that food in there before your arm goes numb." Patty hugged Chelsea and then Serenity did as well. "We'll see you tomorrow, I'm sure."

"Bye, Patty. Serenity, you and Gideon be careful driving back."

"We will. Thanks!" They waved and entered the elevator.

Chelsea maneuvered through the maze of hallways to arrive at Laurie's hospital room. She knocked lightly.

"Come on in."

Laurie's voice sounded strained. The beeping monitors welcomed Chelsea as she held up the bag. "I come bearing gifts."

Tuck practically launched himself out of the chair he was sitting in and strode toward her, relieving her of the food. "God bless you. This hospital food doesn't cut it."

Laurie laughed and then grimaced, cradling her stomach. "He's been complaining about the food here all day long. It's not that bad."

Tuck pointed at the large "Daisy Belle's Diner" printed on the outside of the bag. "Compared to Daisy's food?"

"Point taken." Laurie shifted slightly and flinched. Tuck helped her rearrange the IV and blood pressure cords. "Did you tell Daisy we were here?"

Chelsea wrinkled her nose. "I wasn't sure if I should tell people or not. I didn't want to steal your thunder. But she was so busy I didn't have the opportunity."

Tuck took the lid off a container of vegetable beef soup, retrieved a spoon, and set it on the tray in front of Laurie. "If Daisy knew, she'd have insisted on delivering this food herself."

They all had a good laugh but Chelsea had no doubt he was right. It was Daisy who'd helped Laurie when someone broke into her photography studio and shoved her to the ground. Laurie had a sprained ankle, and Daisy took her to the diner down the street, made her comfortable, and called the police. That was the night Laurie and Tuck met. Daisy liked to take some responsibility for their introduction and treated Laurie like a daughter.

Laurie took a sip of the soup and nodded appreciatively. "Oh yeah. There's no comparing hospital food with this."

Tuck opened a smaller bag with homemade rolls and polished one off in three bites. "Thanks, Chelsea. We appreciate this. It looks like there's plenty. Have you eaten yet?"

Laurie pointed at another empty chair. "Sit, girl. Tell us about your day and have some food."

Chelsea wasn't about to tell them how upset Parker was when she showed up to work late. It'd make Laurie feel horrible and there was no need for that. She shrugged and busied herself with a roast beef sandwich. "How's your little guy?"

Laurie seemed happy, though there was no missing the exhaustion on her face or the concern in her eyes. "He's better. He's doing well on C-PAP but they haven't had any luck switching him off that. They're waiting to see how his oxygen levels are doing and may try again tomorrow. I've been pumping all day so hopefully I'll be able to feed him when he's to that point." The corners of her mouth fell.

Laurie hadn't been shy about how much she'd hoped to have her son with no medication and wanted desperately to breastfeed him. Chelsea could only imagine how she was feeling now.

"We're all praying for him. You'll be holding him and feeding him in no time."

Tuck nodded his agreement. He exchanged a glance with Laurie who tipped her chin. "We named him. We've been telling people as they come by, but will call and let everyone else know tonight."

Chelsea clapped, almost dropping her sandwich. If that bad boy landed on the hospital floor, there'd be no hope of recovery. "Yay! What is it?"

"Nicholas Liam Chandler." As Tuck uttered the words, his voice became husky.

Chelsea caught Laurie wiping a tear from the corner of her eye. "That's a beautiful name. Liam. That was your father's name, wasn't it?"

Tuck nodded and cleared his throat. "And Nicholas was my grandfather's."

"It's perfect. I'm sure both men would be proud. I'll bet Patty and Grams are over the moon."

Laurie chuckled and winced. "They both cried so hard, I didn't think they would ever let go of Tuck's neck."

Chelsea thought of her baby nephew — of Nicholas — and couldn't wait until she got to hold him.

A half hour later, Chelsea knew she should probably get going and let her sister rest. A nurse had come by with some pain medication, and it didn't look like it'd take long for Laurie to fall asleep. Chelsea sure didn't want to leave them, though. But she gave both Laurie and Tuck hugs, promising to come by the next day with some of Laurie's favorite iced tea.

The elevator opened up on the bottom floor of the hospital when something snagged Chelsea's attention. She turned and caught sight of Parker's dog as he disappeared into an elevator across the hallway from her. Parker? What was he doing here? The elevator went up to the second floor and stopped. Curiosity got the best of her and she got back into the elevator she'd just exited and pushed the button for floor number two. The door slid open and she stepped onto the pediatric wing.

*What are you doing, Chels? You should go on home.*

But a need to satisfy her curiosity drove her into the waiting area and then down the hall.

The image of Parker sitting on the floor with five children, smiling and laughing while they played with Happy, stopped her cold. The kids were excited and Parker... Wow, when he really smiled, it completely transformed his face. He looked like a different man and years younger. Seriously handsome. No wonder he'd gotten big-name endorsements before his accident with his roping skills, those muscles befitting a rancher, and that knock down grin...

His gaze shifted from one of the kids to Chelsea. She caught her breath as his frown returned. Disbelief followed by anger and finally curiosity took turns as they marched across his face. He stood quickly, spoke to the nurse nearby, and headed her way.

# Chapter Eight

What was Chelsea doing here? Parker regretted how upset he'd made her this morning and then proceeded to beat himself up over it through the course of the day. Coming here to the hospital was finally the respite he needed from a horrendous Monday. Seeing *her* here was the last thing he'd expected. He told Nurse Kay he'd be back in a moment, and she assured him Happy would be looked after.

As Parker approached Chelsea, he had no idea what she was thinking. She'd averted her eyes, concentrating on a nurse walking by and then watching Happy and the children behind him. After what seemed like forever, she lifted her eyes to his.

"The kids are having a blast with Happy."

He nodded. "Nurse Kay says they look forward to our visit all week."

"You come here every Monday?" Chelsea sounded surprised.

And why shouldn't she be? Especially after today.

He imagined most people would warn children to stay away from someone like him. He didn't know whether he could adequately explain how coming here was mutually beneficial for both him and the kids he saw. He wasn't entirely sure of it himself.

"What are you doing here?" His voice came out somewhat accusing, even though that hadn't been his intention.

Her eyes widened slightly before her frown deepened and she clasped her hands in front of her. "I'm visiting my sister. She and her husband had their baby boy early this morning. He was born seven weeks early and is in the NICU."

Chelsea's words delivered a powerful kick to Parker's conscience. After all that, she'd still come to work. And he'd berated her over being late. Wow, talk about a first-class jerk.

What's more, she could've followed him out of the barn and yelled at him. Accused him for being the horrible person he was. She might have chosen to call his mom and tell her how poorly Parker had acted. Chelsea could've walked out on the job completely.

But she hadn't. She'd stuck with it. Why? To show him she couldn't be pushed around? Or did she need the job as badly as she'd said she did? He still didn't understand why she was working at the ranch in the first place. Yet she'd made it through the mud and then the isolation. Her determination was admirable.

He cleared his throat. "How's the baby doing?"

"Nicholas is strong. Holding his own." Chelsea's voice was tinged with pride. "He'll be okay. But it sounds like he's going to be here for a while. It's hard on my sister and brother-in-law."

Parker could only imagine. "I hope he gets strong soon so he can go home."

Chelsea nodded once. She looked like she might leave but then her gaze focused on the kids behind Parker. "Why do you visit here?"

Parker briefly considered avoiding the question entirely. After what he'd said this morning, he at least owed her some honesty.

The sounds of the kids laughing floated down the hall. "It makes them happy. I'm a sucker for a kid's smile." He realized he was smiling himself when he looked at her again. He hadn't been completely honest with her. "I find some solace here, too, I suppose." He shrugged, not willing to delve into the subject any further.

Chelsea took in his face and her features softened. "Let me guess. This was where you were going when I spilled tea on Happy."

Parker surprised himself by chuckling. "Yes, it was. But don't worry, if his paws were sticky, the kids didn't notice."

"I'm glad."

Her eyes sparkled when she beamed back at him. The green reminded him of the fields at the ranch during the spring. Rich. Lively. Full of understanding. He suddenly wanted to fall into those eyes and find out more about the beautiful woman standing in front of him.

There were more reasons than he could count for why he should take that thought and toss it right out the window. There's no way she'd give him a chance after he was so nasty this morning.

What did she think when she saw his face? Repulsion? Pity? Even if she was one of the few who didn't immediately judge him by the blemishes, she as much as told him that his attitude put her off. Probably put a lot of people off. He didn't deserve her consideration anyway. God knew she could do much better than him.

And if his relationship with Brenda taught him one thing, it was that he couldn't fully trust anyone. He'd thought she was the one for him. He'd even considered proposing to her. Until she dumped him the moment his status as a rodeo star crumbled around him. Knowing what he did now, it was best that she'd walked away. But she'd taken his confidence in women right along with her.

Who's to say Chelsea wasn't just like Brenda, working at the ranch so she could get close to the family money? The moment the thought went through his mind, he knew that wasn't the case. Chelsea had been at the hospital until early this morning, was berated at work, and yet was still here helping her sister at the end of the day. That spoke of commitment and integrity. He doubted Brenda had ever possessed much of either.

Parker felt himself drawn to Chelsea in a powerful way, as if she held the lone candle in a room of darkness. The idea scared him to no end. He coughed and broke their eye contact. "I'd better get back. Happy can get pretty riled up if I'm not there to keep his paws on the ground."

"I'll bet." Amusement lifted a corner of her mouth. "Have a good evening."

"You, too."

She walked away from him and got into the elevator. As the doors closed, his heart squeezed. A part of him wanted to follow her. To say something else to express how sorry he was for his words that morning. But he knew that no matter what he said, he'd make a mess of it. It was better to let it go. Better for both of them.

"Is everything okay?"

Nurse Kay's voice brought Parker's attention back to the kids.

"Sorry about that. Yes, I'm fine." He titled his head toward the giggles and barks. "I'd better get him calmed down before he begins racing down the hall again."

They both laughed at the memory from several weeks ago. But Parker's mind continued to focus on Chelsea and the way vulnerability and strength mixed together to create a mystery he felt inexplicably drawn to solve.

~

Chelsea still couldn't wrap her mind around the image of Parker at the children's ward last night. Seriously, if someone had asked her to guess what he did in his spare time, making sick children happy wouldn't have even made a ripple in the pond.

She thought she had Parker figured out. Had him categorized in her head. Now she didn't know where to put him.

When she got to the ranch the next morning, there was no sign of Parker. Chelsea walked up the stairs to her office, surprised to find the light had been turned on. She put her stuff down and turned to the desk, stopping in her tracks.

Sitting there was a piece of paper and a bottle of the blueberry tea she liked.

Chelsea blinked twice before walking forward to lift the paper off the smooth surface of the desk. The note was short and written in Parker's flowing print.

*Chelsea,*

*Please forgive my rudeness yesterday morning. I should have given you the opportunity to explain. If you need time off to help your sister and her family, don't hesitate to ask. I hope your nephew continues to improve daily.*

*Regards,*
*Parker*

Chelsea read it three times before placing it on the desk again. She grasped the tea, surprised to find it was ice cold. Parker had to have left it minutes before she arrived.

And he'd remembered what kind of tea she liked from that morning at the gas station. That meant as much as anything else.

She twisted the top off the bottle and took a drink. The realization that he'd paid so much attention brought a smile to her lips.

"Okay, Mr. Wilson. I'll accept your offer of a truce."

Chelsea sipped on her tea most of the morning as she worked. She didn't hear a peep from Parker or anyone else. By lunch time, she couldn't wait to get outside for a few minutes. She heated up some leftover pizza in the microwave then headed down from the barn until she came to what had become her favorite tree. It overlooked the pasture which, at this moment, was moving slightly in the breeze and reminded her of waves on the ocean. She tried to imagine what it would all look like once spring had really started to set in. Green grass, the tree filled with leaves. It'd be gorgeous.

The new longhorns were gone now. They must have been relocated to the rest of the herd. None of them were visible from her location, and Chelsea missed watching them.

She settled onto the ground at the base of the tree and leaned her back against the trunk. It was a warm day compared to the last week, and she was grateful to soak in some sunshine. It didn't take long to polish off her pizza. She was so relaxed that when something scampered out of the brush, she jumped, scraping her back on the bark. "Ouch!"

A small, black kitten leapt into the air and bounced away from Chelsea, apparently as shocked as she was.

Chelsea placed a hand on her lower back, rubbing at the spot she'd hurt. Now that she knew it was just a kitten, she willed her heart to calm down. She held her other hand out toward the tiny animal and clicked her tongue.

The kitten watched her for a moment, the hair on the back of its neck smoothing into place. It tentatively approached her. And then, as if the air of caution were a façade, trotted right up to sniff Chelsea's fingers.

The whiskers tickled and Chelsea fought to keep her hand still. Within moments, the kitten was rubbing its face against her hand while she scratched its ears. It wasn't until the kitten had rolled onto its back that Chelsea saw it was a girl.

The kitten must have decided she was all right because she climbed into Chelsea's lap and curled up against her stomach, purrs vibrating as the cat breathed in and out.

"Just make yourself comfortable, why don't you? Shouldn't you be in a barn somewhere catching a mouse or two?"

A deep voice to Chelsea's left startled her. Good grief, for not having seen a soul all morning, apparently she was in Grand Central Station now. "That's probably Patch's kitten. We were able to rehome all but one of them." Parker tilted his head toward the fuzz ball. "Every time someone comes to adopt her, she's nowhere to be found."

Since Parker was standing, Chelsea had to tilt her head way back to see him. "Maybe she doesn't want to leave."

"Could be." Parker put his hands in the pockets of his jeans and studied something in the distance.

The silence was odd. Not entirely uncomfortable. Chelsea cupped the kitten's sweet little face in her hand. "Thanks for the tea. And the note." She fought to keep her gaze on the small animal. "I doubt I'll need any extra time off. My brother-in-law has a lot of family in the area. They probably have more help than they want right now."

"That's good they have so much support."

Chelsea thought he was going to leave. Instead, he lowered himself onto a nearby rock and stretched his long legs out in front of him. What was she supposed to say?

She studied his profile. His strong jaw appeared clenched, but relaxed as the minutes ticked by. The breeze blew his brown hair and the blue sky reflected in his hazel eyes. This was the most laidback she'd ever seen him, short of that small glimpse at the hospital.

"It's neat that you go visit the kids at the hospital like you do. I'm sure it makes a big difference to them."

Parker gave a little shrug. "I hope it helps them as much as it helps me." They sat in silence for a while before he turned his gaze on the now-sleeping kitten in her lap. "She likes you. Maybe you should keep her."

"Oh, I couldn't. I'm renting the apartment above my sister's photography studio. She'd kill me if I brought an animal in." Maybe a slight exaggeration, but Laurie probably wouldn't approve. And with everything going on right now with Nicholas, Chelsea wasn't about to place any additional stress on her. She ran a finger along the kitten's nose. "She is sweet, though."

"Do you eat lunch out here often?"

"Most days." Anxiety squeezed her chest. "I hope that's okay."

Parker nodded. "This is one of my favorite spots on the ranch. You have good taste."

Chelsea shifted to rest her back and the kitten did, too. "Are the new yearlings with the rest of the herd now?"

"Yes. They seem to be transitioning well. They'll all be fine once they figure out the pecking order."

"That's good. I miss getting to watch them, though." She paused. "This place is beautiful. I look out at that field and it's like all is right with the world." Too bad that wasn't the case. She thought about Nicholas and then about her parents coming. That last one brought tension back into her shoulders. So much for the relaxation lasting long. She glanced at the clock on her phone. "I'd better get back to the office."

She picked the kitten up as she stood, petting the animal's head before setting her back down on the grass.

Parker stood as well, his hands going right back into his pockets. "Listen, about those files I wanted you to finish scanning? Don't worry about those. I'm sure you're just about sick of messing with them."

*Boy, he could say that again.* "It's getting pretty old."

"Leave them be, and I'll have them carted out of your office tonight. I've got a full afternoon today. But tomorrow, we can go see how the new longhorns are integrating into the herd. If that's something you're interested in."

The thought of having the opportunity to watch the longhorns up close sounded fun. "I'd like that."

"Good. I'll be by to pick you up outside the barn at ten tomorrow morning." He gave her a short nod and turned, walking away from her.

"I'll be ready. Thank you."

He lifted a hand in a half wave and left. The man was an enigma. His stride and the way he carried himself suggested he was not only confident, but completely sure of his place in life and with what he was doing on the ranch. At the same time, there was a thread of uncertainty when he interacted with her. Was it only with her, or was it with people in general?

She had a feeling that uncertainty was relatively new. Had it come into play after his accident? She found herself wishing she'd had the opportunity to meet him two or three years ago. To see what he was like when he was roping. Or even earlier — when he was growing up on the ranch. She'd be willing to bet he was the kind of boy that was into everything. She imagined him trailing his father as they checked on the livestock.

Yes, Parker gave the impression of someone who had had to overcome many challenges in his life. Which made Chelsea even more curious about him.

# Chapter Nine

Parker had a hard time getting the vision of Chelsea sitting on the edge of the pasture out of his head. With the way her hair had draped over her shoulder and the gentle way she cradled the kitten, the scene would have made the perfect portrait. He could suddenly see it hanging above the fireplace in the sitting room.

He shook away the thought. The last thing he needed was to imagine Chelsea in his home in any way, shape, or form. It didn't matter how green her eyes were. Or how her smile somehow sped up the tempo of his heart, while simultaneously frustrating him.

He was distracted and he didn't notice Mom until she spoke just behind his shoulder.

"Is everything okay?"

"Yeah, Mom. I'm fine. It's been a long week." He'd let his guard down. He needed to be more careful. Ever since the accident, he'd worked hard to not give his mom a reason to worry about him.

"I completely understand. Things are moving

forward nicely for Kara's wedding. Less than three weeks to go."

Mom paused as though she were waiting for him to comment. His stomach clenched, and he could swear the temperature in the room had jumped ten degrees. His date. It'd been the furthest thing from his mind since he'd last spoken to his mom about it. Where was he going to find someone in less than three weeks? It was better to deflect than broach the subject and nothing would swerve her attention like the bride-to-be. "I haven't seen Kara much, but every time I do, she looks blissful."

"She's excited. I'm certain I've seen her floating above the ground more than once." She studied Parker. "Have you asked anyone to accompany you to the wedding?"

So much for changing the subject. It was like wanting to move a mountain with a child's sand shovel. "I haven't. I still have plenty of time."

"Then I shouldn't worry? About that or anything else?"

He knew full well Mom would worry no matter how he answered. "No, you shouldn't." He leaned forward and kissed her cheek. "It's taking a little while to adjust to being on the ranch again, but I'm doing fine."

"Good." Mom squeezed his shoulder. "Your dad would be proud of you. I hope you know that." She kissed him on the cheek.

Parker tried to swallow past the lump that had formed in his throat. He didn't trust his voice and gave her a nod instead.

"You should get some rest. You look exhausted."

"I will." He watched as she disappeared through the doorway.

That he still appeared tired to others around him was frustrating. What he wouldn't give for a full night's sleep without nightmares. He couldn't remember what it was like to be rested. It was crazy that, even a year after his accident, he still felt the physical echoes of his injuries.

True to his expectations, he spent that night alternating between nightmares and dreams where he was almost certain he heard Chelsea's voice. But it was always faint and her face was just out of sight meaning he was never sure whether it was her or not. By the time the sky lightened the next morning, he was sick of trying to get any more sleep.

Parker busied himself with the long list of things he needed to get done. Anything to keep himself from counting down the minutes until he picked up Chelsea at the barn. Every time he relaxed and let his mind wander, her face would appear. Often, he'd remember the hurt in her eyes when he berated her the other morning. Or that flash of fire when he'd angered her. But most of the time, it was the softness while she was holding the kitten and talking to him as if she didn't hate him.

He had no business picturing her face at all, though. And maybe that was what bothered him more than anything else. It was as though the woman was intent on exasperating him even when she wasn't around, which was ridiculous. But it sounded good and was a lot better than analyzing the reasons why he felt that way in the first place.

At exactly ten o'clock, he drove up in front of the barn to find her waiting for him. She was sitting on the steps, her cell phone in hand, and joy on her face. Parker rolled his window down. "Good news?"

Chelsea hopped up from the steps, jogged around the front of the truck, and slid into the passenger seat. She held the phone out, and he could see the photo of a tiny baby sleeping, an oxygen tube taped under his nose.

"They were able to take Nicholas off C-PAP this morning. He'll probably receive oxygen through the cannula for a while. But it meant Laurie got to really hold him for the first time." Her voice caught, and she focused on her phone, flipping through an album to show him another picture.

The red-headed woman holding the infant was grinning. If Parker saw the two of them together in person, he wouldn't have guessed them to be sisters.

"That's great news. I'm happy for you all. He's a handsome baby."

"Thanks!" Chelsea turned the phone off and slid it into her back pocket. "I can't wait to hold the little guy myself."

Parker wanted to ask her if she hoped to have children of her own one day, but it was an entirely inappropriate question. Instead, he drove the truck to the far side of the pasture where the longhorns were located. He jabbed a thumb behind them. "I'm bringing something for the longhorns. They know the sound of this truck so keep an eye on the pasture ahead as we get closer."

Chelsea leaned forward in her seat as she took in the passing landscape. They rounded a grove of trees. Parker immediately spotted the herd. The moment they noticed his truck, the whole lot of them ran. He pointed them out. "Right there. See them?"

"Wow! Look at them go."

Parker stopped the truck near the fence line and got

out. Before he had a chance to open the door for her, Chelsea was jogging around the truck to his location.

The longhorns approached, dirt flying into the air behind them.

"They know I have treats for them," Parker said. "Wait right here." He walked to the back of the pickup and retrieved the bucket of range cubes before rejoining Chelsea. "This is what they're running for."

"It's not because they're excited to have visitors, then?" Chelsea grinned as the herd approached in anticipation. "They really are magnificent when they run. How many do you have again?"

"There are twenty-two here. We have another thirteen in a separate area. Most of them are calves going through the weaning process and some steers." Parker approached the metal fence and reached a hand through to pat the head of the largest animal. "This is Sebastian, our bull. He's one of the first to insist on getting a treat."

Sebastian turned his head sideways and tried to stick his nose through the slats in the fencing. His horns clanged against the metal.

Parker noted that Chelsea still stood where he left her but she seemed interested in the cattle. "You can come closer if you want to. Stay far enough back to avoid getting grazed by a horn." One of Sebastian's horns came through again, and Parker took a step backwards. "Like that." He laughed.

He had spent little time out here since coming back. There were too many memories of Dad. But now, showing Chelsea, it felt different. New. The cattle probably recognized the ranch truck and expected the treats more than anything. Even if it was silly, part of Parker hoped they somehow sensed that he used to spend hours out here watching over the herd when he was a teenager.

"Is everything okay?"

Parker hadn't even noticed that Chelsea had walked forward until she was right behind him. When he turned, her eyes brimmed with concern.

"Yeah. I'm fine." He didn't want to say anything, but there was something about Chelsea that brought the words out anyway. "I used to work out here with my dad when I was a kid."

"You miss him. Your dad."

The truth of her words slammed Parker hard in the chest. This was why he'd avoided the ranch. Yet, strangely, he felt closer to Dad right now than he had in a long time. He nodded once. "We did everything together. The ranch was never the same without him."

"Is that why you left?"

Parker turned and pinned her with a curious glance. "You been checking on me?"

Chelsea had the good sense to blush. She gave a little shrug. "I might have Googled your name last week." The red deepened. "Or, you know, Googled your ranch." The words stumbled over each other.

She was embarrassed. The red looked good on her. She stuck her hands into the pockets of her heavy coat and shuffled her feet — still clad in those ridiculous boots. With the form-fitting jeans she was wearing, all she needed was a good pair of cowgirl boots and she'd really look like she belonged here with him.

The thought kicked his heart rate into high gear. Where had that come from?

Did *he* even belong here anymore?

This conversation was diving into the personal fast. It was time to change the subject. "Do you want to feed Sebastian?"

Chelsea's eyes widened and her face looked comical. "Oh, no. I'm fine right here, thank you."

Parker shrugged. "You don't know what you're missing." With that, he got a treat out of the bucket and held it out to Sebastian. The bull didn't hesitate to stretch his long tongue out, take the treat from his hand, and munch away. Dirt and spittle were all that the bull left behind. Parker wiped his hand off on his jeans. It only took moments for Sebastian to stick his tongue back out for a second sample.

Chelsea chuckled. "He sure likes those, doesn't he? What's in it?"

"Protein, fat, fiber, and minerals. It's a good supplement. We put salt and mineral blocks where they can get to them, too. But the range cubes are especially popular." Parker took a handful and tossed them over the railing. Several of the animals crowded to get a piece, including two of the calves.

"They're adorable." Chelsea was smiling at the calves.

"I'd offer for you to feed them, but they tend to be more nervous." He pointed to five heifers that were keeping more of a distance between them and the rest of the herd. "Those are the five that came in last week."

She studied them and frowned. "Are they choosing to separate themselves, or are the others leaving them out?"

"This is a pretty common reaction. It's a little of both. They're doing well, but it may take a while for them to integrate into the rest of the herd completely. Most of them do. Every once in a while, you'll see a group that remains independent — almost like a mini herd within the herd." A brindle pushed her way forward and stuck her nose through the railing. "This is Sadie, our matriarch." He reached a hand through to pat her head. "The black heifer calf is hers."

Chelsea edged a little closer, her back straight as if she were willing herself to appear confident. She stopped several feet away from the animals. Parker put a hand on her lower back and ushered her forward. Then, with a boldness that surprised even him, he took her hand and placed it on Sadie's head. He didn't expect the intense sensations that shot straight to his chest at the contact with her skin. His heart skipped a beat.

Chelsea's hand trembled. Had she felt it, too? Doubtful. Surely the shiver came from patting the animal she'd been afraid of. He kept his hand over hers — telling himself it was only to ease her trepidation. Sadie shifted and Chelsea jerked her hand back. Parker missed the way her soft skin felt against his. He leaned down to get a range cube and gave it to her. "Hold it on the palm of your hand. Sadie's gentle, trust me."

She took the cube and tentatively held her hand out. Sadie didn't hesitate to poke her nose through the railing and curl her tongue around the treat, sweeping it into her mouth.

Chelsea jumped a little and wrinkled her nose. "Her tongue is like a warm slug." She shook her hand and then wiped it on her jeans before seeking the warmth of her jacket pockets.

Did she have any idea just how cute she looked right now with her nose still creased a bit? Parker knew he was grinning like a crazy guy and had to fight to rein in his response. His thoughts flew to Brenda. She wouldn't have stepped foot on the ranch, much less gotten up the courage to feed Sadie. He doubted anything but a pile of money would've changed her mind on the subject. Yet Chelsea had pushed past her fear... why? Because he'd asked her to? Because she was curious about Sadie? Whatever the reason, her bravery impressed him.

"They have the kindest eyes."

Chelsea's words broke Parker's reverie. He had no business comparing the two women. Chelsea worked for his family. Worked for the ranch. But when she turned her gaze on him, Parker couldn't agree with her more. However, it wasn't the animal's eyes he was taken with, but rather those belonging to the beautiful woman standing in front of him.

Chelsea may not understand what goes on with a ranch, but there was a lot more to her than he'd admitted. He wanted to know more about her. Wanted to know why she was determined to keep this job, even when her employer was a jerk.

Now he knew watching the cattle made her smile. Oh, and apparently some blueberry tea.

Despite his every attempt to remain neutral on the topic of Chelsea Blake, he had an irrational need to discover what else might light up those expressive eyes of hers.

~

"What?!" Chelsea's voice came out more like a squeak. It was Thursday evening and she'd stopped by the hospital to hold her baby nephew for the first time. The tiny form in her arms stretched before bringing his knees up to his chest. Nicholas's lips made little suckling noises before he fell back to sleep again. Chelsea cringed as she tried to shove down the panic that was rising in her chest. "They'll be here tomorrow night?"

Even though their parents had promised they'd come spend several months in Kitner after the baby's birth, Chelsea always had a hard time imagining them actually making good on their word. Oh sure, she'd been preparing for it with her new job and everything. Truthfully, in the back of her mind, she'd half expected them to never show up at all.

Now they were coming to town tomorrow. Less than twenty-four hours from now. Not only that, but she'd have a full two days over the weekend to hang out with them before escaping back to the ranch. Oh yeah, this would be fun.

The only thing that eased her serious case of the nerves was watching the sweet face of her nephew. Laurie and Tuck might have to wrangle him from her arms before she left. Everything about him was perfect. From the baby smell to that tiny nose. Not to mention the smallest tuft of red hair on his head, something Tuck liked to comment on and make Laurie blush over. But Chelsea could tell her sister was thrilled.

Chelsea ran a thumb lightly over Nicholas's soft hand. She tried to imagine Mom holding him and couldn't. Come to think of it, she couldn't imagine her mom doing anything maternal. "Are they staying with you guys?"

"Thank goodness, no." Laurie's eyes widened. "We offered because it was the right thing to do. And if they'd taken us up on it, it would've been fine." The look she exchanged with Tuck told Chelsea volumes. "But they insisted on staying at the Hilton downtown."

For three months? But then, that was Henry and

Cadence Blake. They had plenty of money and didn't mind spending it. That's what money was for, though, right? Besides, the doctors said Nicholas would be at the hospital for several days still. Possibly more, since every time they removed the extra oxygen, his O2 levels dropped. He needed to keep those levels up before he could go home. He was having a difficult time maintaining his body temperature, too.

"Well, that's good. They'll be comfortable there and only five minutes or so from your house."

"Exactly." Laurie nodded but said nothing else.

Chelsea knew her older sister was as nervous to see their parents as she was. But talking about it till they were blue in the face didn't help. Goodness knows they'd tried it before.

Nicholas made a little squeak, his eyes opening just wide enough to show off their dark blue color.

Chelsea studied his serene little face. He'd had to deal with a lot in the four days since his birth, and yet he had complete trust in the people around him. Why couldn't she be more like him? Why couldn't she trust that God knew what He was doing? Maybe her persistence and work would speak for themselves when it came to their parents.

She could do this. She could see her parents tomorrow, visit with them, enjoy the reunion, and not let it get to her. *You're going to have to grant me a huge helping of patience, Lord.*

Chelsea thought Nicholas might go back to sleep, but he turned his head to the side and tried to suck on her arm. "Sorry, little guy. I can't do much to help you there." He voiced his frustration.

Tuck chuckled and scooped his little boy into his arms, being careful to keep the oxygen tube from getting tangled. He pressed a kiss to the baby's forehead and placed him in Laurie's arms. She nuzzled him before trying to get him to latch on to eat.

Breastfeeding had proven difficult so far, but Laurie told Chelsea she was determined to make it work. And already, Nicholas was doing better with it.

Once Nicholas was eating contentedly, Laurie focused on Chelsea.

"So, are you meeting us for dinner tomorrow night after they arrive?"

Chelsea leaned her head against the back of her chair. Well, that surge of confidence had lasted an entire forty-five seconds.

"Yes, I'll be there. What time?"

"Call me when you get off work. I still don't know what time they're getting into town. I wish we could eat here, but they insisted we go out because it's too germy in the hospital, and I'm not up to fixing a big meal at home yet."

Chelsea didn't blame her. "Yeah, that sounds good." Right up there with going to the dentist. Or walking around in the mud barefoot. She'd probably take the mud over dinner with her parents anytime.

Her mind went to the ranch. What was Parker up to? She thought about how he'd insisted she push past her fear of feeding Sadie. Chelsea could still feel the way the heifer's tongue had curled around her hand. Never in her life would she have guessed that, one day, she'd have fun feeding a range cube to a longhorn.

Parker had been different today. He seemed to have fun, something that'd looked good on him. More importantly, he'd relaxed around her. Chelsea suspected there were few people he did that with and it made her feel special, whether she should or not.

When she first started this job, she'd dreaded going to the ranch. Now, she was anticipating her return to work tomorrow.

"What are you smiling about?" Laurie spoke from the bed, a knowing look on her face.

Chelsea schooled her features and tried for her best uninterested shrug. "I have no idea what you're talking about."

"Mmmm hmmm."

## Chapter Ten

Parker had kept busy out at one of the stock ponds, beginning repairs to the small dock that ran along one side. He had many memories of jumping off that dock and going swimming when he was a kid. He and Kara had fun swinging from the rope that hung from a tree along the bank. The rope was still there, although it was tattered from years of sun and bad weather.

Parker took Happy to the stock pond frequently. In March, it was still too cold for even the dog to go swimming, but it was one of Parker's favorite places to walk.

The other day, as he'd stepped onto the dock, one board had collapsed right under him. He'd managed to catch himself before twisting an ankle, but he hadn't realized the dock had fallen into such disrepair. Upon further inspection, he discovered most of the boards desperately needed to be replaced.

Normally, a project like this was something he welcomed. It meant he could stay busy on the ranch, in close range if needed, but manage to avoid contact with anyone else if that's what he wanted.

And usually, that was exactly what he would've chosen to do.

Now it was Friday morning and he was back at the stock pond again, laying out the next planks to hammer into place. Instead of the usual peace he enjoyed, his mind kept wandering to Chelsea.

He didn't see her at all yesterday. Had no real reason to run into her today, either. She had plenty of things to do and if, for some reason she needed to contact him, she had his cell phone number.

Then why did he keep seeing her face when he stared at the water? He let his gaze wander the bank of the pond, pausing at one of the large trees. The image of Chelsea sitting beneath a tree, black kitten in her lap, was so vivid it was as though he had taken a mental photograph.

Parker looked at his watch. It was nearly lunchtime. Would she be there again?

Did it matter?

As if to answer his own question, he picked up his hammer and slammed a nail into the board with way more force than was necessary. Happy trotted over, sat on the same board, and stared at Parker expectantly.

"You'd better move, buddy. We still have several hours of work to go."

Happy stared at him, not a muscle twitching.

Parker sat back and shook his head. "What's your deal?"

Happy laid down then, resting his chin on his paws.

Apparently, the dog knew it was time to eat and would not take no for an answer.

"Fine. Let's go." Parker stood and made a wide

motion toward the truck. Happy got there before he did. Normally, Parker would sit on the tailgate and eat the sandwich he'd brought. But again, all he could picture was Chelsea eating lunch alone under one of his favorite trees.

In direct contrast to his good sense, he opened the cab of the truck and Happy hopped inside. Parker got his bowl of dog food and set it on the floorboard. Happy took little time to gobble it all up. Tired from all the running and exploring he'd been doing, he immediately curled up on the passenger seat and was asleep before Parker had gotten halfway across the ranch.

As he neared the tree, he saw Chelsea resting against the trunk. He leaned forward toward the steering wheel as his heart rate quickened. Her chin lifted when he pulled up not far away and turned off the engine. Happy took in his surroundings, sighed, and went back to sleep.

Parker got his lunch box from the back seat of the truck, rolled the window down a little, and left Happy to nap in peace as he got out.

Chelsea straightened. She had a sandwich in her hand and she set it back down on a paper towel resting on the grass beside her. She pulled her phone from her back pocket and turned on the screen. "Did I miss a call from you?"

"No." What was he doing here? She looked almost panicked wondering if he'd tried to contact her about a job and she'd missed it somehow. What did that say about how she thought of him? Considering how he'd treated her most of the time she'd been at the ranch, he couldn't say he blamed her. Parker held up his lunch. "I was going to stop and eat. I think I mentioned before that this was one of my favorite places on the ranch."

"Oh!" Chelsea rushed to her feet, knocking her bottle of tea over. Luckily, the lid was screwed on tight and none of it spilled. She righted the bottle and put it back in a bag. "I'll just pack this up so you can enjoy your lunch."

Okay, that hadn't exactly gone the way he intended it to. Parker strode forward and took the lunch bag from Chelsea to get her to stop feverishly stuffing items into it. "I thought I might join you."

Chelsea tilted her head to one side, her mouth slightly open. She pressed her lips together, blinked several times, and reached for her bag. "Are you sure? I don't mind leaving."

"I'm positive." Parker waited for her to sit down but she didn't move a muscle. He needed to make the first move. He settled onto the nearby rock and retrieved his lunch items. Midway through, he noticed Chelsea sitting back down in his periphery.

The turkey sandwich hit the spot, and he'd consumed half of it before breaking for a drink. Meanwhile, Chelsea hadn't said a word. She kept her eyes on the pasture in the distance. Some of the longhorns had wandered into the area, content to graze in the sun.

Last time they'd sat here together, she'd relaxed against the tree trunk. Even though she'd seemed wary of him, she'd at least conversed. He thought they'd gotten along well when he took her to see the longhorns. And she'd thanked him for the tea and note. Surely she wasn't angry with him. At least not for anything new.

He scratched his forehead at the hairline. It wasn't

until Chelsea released a heavy sigh that he ventured to speak. "Is something wrong?"

Her gaze snapped to his. She shifted her position on the grass, her shoulders slumping. At that moment, the black kitten from the other day pounced out of a bush and onto a leaf. Chelsea's face broke into a smile as she gathered the kitten onto her lap. "Hey, there. I'd wondered where you'd gone."

The transformation from a ball of nerves to relaxed happened so quickly, Parker was left staring at her. He listened as Chelsea spoke to the kitten like she might have an old friend. Her tone of voice, her posture, it was all very different from when she spoke to him. Did he make her that uncomfortable? The possibility bothered him to no end.

Chelsea continued to pet the kitten but turned to him, her lashes lifting to reveal green eyes awash with conflict. "My parents are coming into town tonight."

"I take it that's not a good thing."

She shrugged. "Let me put it this way. I called to tell them my sister was in early labor last Friday. I had to leave a message. They didn't bother calling back until yesterday. One week later."

That was unusually cold. He was sure there was more to the situation, but hesitated to push her by asking too many questions.

Chelsea took another bite of her sandwich, pinched off a piece of meat to give to the kitten, then stuffed it back in her bag. She'd barely eaten any. Everything — from the way she worked her jaw to the fact she'd chewed on her lip enough to draw blood — illustrated the immense amount of stress she was under.

Parker had a thought. "I know how hard it is to focus when you're worried about something. Believe me." He paused. Was he willing to break his bubble of solitude? The sadness on her face convinced him. "When we're done eating, why don't you come help me with a project on the other side of the ranch."

Her eyebrows shot upwards. "What is this project we'll be working on?"

"You'll find out when we get there." He popped the last bite of his sandwich in his mouth, dusted off his hands, and stood. "Are you coming?"

The kitten batted at her lunch bag until Chelsea picked it up and held it out of reach. "Yes, I'll come with you."

~

Chelsea wasn't in the mood for company. But that slightly mischievous glint in Parker's eyes got the best of her and she knew she'd wonder what this project was all day if she didn't go see for herself. When she set the kitten down and stood, she swore she saw a grin on his face before he'd turned and headed toward the truck.

She gathered up her stuff, jogged to the passenger door, and began to climb in when Happy stood on the seat and wagged his little tail. "I didn't know you were in here."

"He was taking his mid-day nap. Closely followed by the afternoon nap, late afternoon nap, and the evening nap."

Despite her poor mood, Chelsea chuckled. "Do I need to ride in the bed of the truck. Is this your spot?"

As if he knew what she was saying, Happy shook himself and then hopped into the tiny backseat. Chelsea quickly claimed the vacated spot and put her seatbelt on. She wanted to ask again where they were going but knew better not to. If there was one thing she'd figured out about Parker, it was that he didn't converse unless it was necessary.

Today, that suited her fine.

The scenery went by as he drove across the ranch. She couldn't believe that less than two weeks ago, she'd dreaded coming to this place. Now she found it one of the most peaceful locations she'd ever known. The pasture, the longhorns, everything about it exuded tranquility. Maybe, one day, she'd own a piece of land herself. Oh, she was kidding herself. She couldn't run something like this. If she was as bad with animals as she was with plants, they wouldn't have a prayer. But a place to go to where there was no one but her and the beauty that God created...

Chelsea gazed beyond the acres and acres of grass to the wall of trees beyond. If she went off exploring, what were the odds she could get lost and not have to go to dinner with her parents tonight? Yeah, the fact it was a little bit tempting wasn't a good sign. Maybe a project to focus on wasn't such a bad idea after all.

Besides, the idea of spending time with Parker appealed to her. Which wasn't necessarily a good thing, either. She wouldn't admit how much she'd thought about their trip to see the longhorns the other day.

Ever since Parker's apology, he'd acted differently. Chelsea had been curious about him before. But now, she felt drawn to him somehow. It wasn't even anything she could explain.

Parker had opened up a little about his dad. He'd come across as vulnerable then. Chelsea sensed he was trying to find his place in life right now, and she could certainly sympathize with that.

The memory of his hand holding hers when they were feeding Sadie rushed to mind and her face heated. She'd worked hard to push those thoughts aside over the last two days, but apparently that hadn't worked.

Yep, she was way too happy about spending time with Parker this afternoon. Not good. Chelsea needed to keep her distance a little. She couldn't afford to fall for her employer, not when she needed this job so badly. There was enough drama going on in her life right now without adding more to it.

A little longer and she might almost convince herself she was right. She gave a mental sigh.

Just when Chelsea was going to ask how much longer they'd be driving, a small pond came into view. She guessed it to be an acre, maybe smaller. A wooden dock — or at least a partial one — ran along a section of it. The whole thing was right out of a summer camp brochure.

Happy whined and stood with his front paws on the console between the two humans.

"He likes it out here," said Parker by way of an explanation.

She could understand why.

Parker pulled up next to the dock and turned off the engine. He opened his door, and she followed suit.

There was a large stack of lumber in one spot. "Are you building this?"

"More like repairing the old one." Parker led the way to the dock. "The previous planks were giving way. I hated to see it fall apart. It's one of the first things my dad built on this property." His voice took on a wistful tone.

Chelsea put a hand above her eyes to block out the high sun and took in the scene. Happy ran along the shore, his paws just out of reach of the water. "Does he hate getting wet?"

A corner of Parker's mouth lifted. "The water's too cold right now. You should see him in the summer. I can't get him out of the water then."

Chelsea had loved to swim when she was kid. She'd nearly forgotten, it'd been such a long time. She remembered going to a resort several times as a family. Well, the four of them plus the nanny. But she and Laurie had gotten to stay up late and swim in the heated pool. It'd been like heaven at the time.

She caught Parker watching her and she blinked away the memories. He'd stepped up onto the part of the dock that had already been completed. By her estimation, there were still dozens of planks left to be placed. "Stress relief, huh?"

Parker shrugged.

Chelsea pointed a finger at him. "If you tell me to sand the floor, I'm walking out of here."

Parker chuckled, his deep voice rolling over her. "No. And while the truck could use a good wash and wax, we will be working on something much more difficult." He bent down to retrieve a pair of hammers from a toolbox at his feet. "We're going to nail some boards." He hefted the tools. "Which one do you want? Blue or red?"

Chelsea pointed to the hammer with the red handle. "Are you going to show me how to drive a nail into the board with one swing?"

"I sure will." Parker puffed out his chest. "As soon as I figure that out myself."

Chelsea laughed. She'd never nailed a thing in her life. How pathetic was that? Dad always hired someone to do any work around their place. The hammer felt completely foreign in her hand. "Okay, Mr. Miyagi, show me how this is done."

Parker picked up a board from the pile and placed it on the two rims of the dock. Then he knelt on the boards that had been secured. "We'll place two nails on each side. I've measured and cut everything so it should come together quickly." He lifted his head to make eye contact with her. "Does that sound good?"

"Sure." She hoped she projected more confidence than she was feeling.

Parker put a box of nails down in the space between them. He took one out of the box, placed it, and drove it into the wood with four strikes of the hammer. He made it look easy.

Chelsea took out a nail, held it with one hand, and raised the hammer above her head. Without warning, she felt a large hand cover her own.

"Hold on. You'll smash your fingers if you do that." With his hand still on top of hers, he lowered the hammer and took it. He scooted over until he was directly behind her, his chest pressed against her back.

Chelsea sucked in a breath and tried to ignore the tendrils of electricity that assaulted her nerves. She could smell the mixture of pine and soap, feel his chest move as he took a breath. What was it he was saying? She shook her head and forced herself to focus.

"Start out with small hits until you've got the nail partly into the wood. Then you can move your hand and hit it harder. Like this." He demonstrated with the nail she'd been holding. He dug another out of the box and passed it to her. "You try."

Taking the nail from him, she willed her hands not to shake. She placed the nail and took the hammer back, their fingers brushing. Her heart pounded in response when he still hadn't moved away from her. She prayed he didn't hear her pulse and tried to mimic what he'd shown her.

"Better!" He took her hand in his again and adjusted it on the handle. "This will make it easier. After a few nails, it'll become second nature."

She finished driving the nail into the wood and looked back at him. He nodded in approval. "I'm pretty sure you'll get done with this a whole lot faster without me."

"Nah. It'll give me time to position the next board." He winked.

They worked in companionable silence for a half hour. True to his word, she got faster over time. Nothing like Parker, though. The guy was a beast. He could get his two nails in, retrieve the next board and have it placed before Chelsea had finished her set. She was definitely slowing him down, though he didn't seem to mind.

"I have to admit, you're right."

Parker stopped mid-swing. "That's something I rarely hear."

Chelsea's lips quirked. "Never mind."

"Sorry, go on." He feigned disinterest, but his eyes never left hers.

"This is therapeutic."

He nodded. "I've always thought so." He hesitated. "I take it you had no building sessions with Daddy Dearest, huh?"

A cynical laugh slipped past her lips before she could put a stop to it. "Oh, he wouldn't have been caught dead doing something like this. He'd hire someone, and then hire someone else to oversee everything to make sure it was done right."

The air between them felt weighted with Parker's curiosity. He didn't say a word, and Chelsea was tempted to stay quiet and let the moment go. She appreciated that he didn't ask more questions. Maybe that's what loosened her tongue. "My parents are wealthy. They have been all my life. I had more things growing up than any one kid should have in a lifetime." Chelsea wiped dirt off her hands. "I had everything except parents who were there for me. They had plans for me and my sister. I thought sticking to those plans would make them proud of me." She swallowed hard. "I was naïve."

# Chapter Eleven

The vulnerability in Chelsea's voice gripped Parker's heart. He set another plank of wood in place and sat down beside her. "And you're working here at the ranch because…"

She shrugged. "Because I need to find out who I am, prove to them I have my own identity outside of being a Blake and their money. My parents enjoy their wealth, and there's nothing wrong with that. But most of the time, it didn't include my sister and me. Most memories I have playing games and being read to include our nannies. All while my parents were out exploring the world during their vacations." She used the nail she was holding to pick at a knot in the wood. "I was a spoiled, rich kid. I didn't know any different and I didn't care."

"What changed?"

Chelsea dropped the nail and waited for it to roll to a stop. "Daddy was grooming me to work for a big law firm in New York. He'd scored me an internship, and I knew he'd been instrumental in getting me that spot.

There were five of us interning that year, all vying for one permanent position with the firm." She let out a humorless laugh. "I thought if I proved myself to the company and got that position, I'd give my dad something to be proud of."

She paused and Parker frowned. "I take it you didn't get the position?"

"I would've. But I was walking past my boss's office, Mr. Sandrove, and I overheard him talking to George, one of the other interns. He told George that he'd get the permanent position if it were up to him. I didn't deserve it, but he had to offer it to me because of my father. That my father had invested so much money into the law firm and expected me to end up in management at some point. Mr. Sandrove was afraid that, if he didn't make me a permanent part of the firm, his job might be in jeopardy."

Parker wanted to say something but didn't have the words. He could imagine overhearing something like that and the devastation it would bring on many different levels.

Chelsea shifted and sat with her legs crossed. "I was angry. I couldn't believe Mr. Sandrove was going to make that kind of decision just so he could appease my dad." She shook her head and frowned. "Then it hit me. I was no different. Every decision I'd made as a teen and young adult was based on whether or not Dad would approve of the outcome. That's when I decided I had to stop being Henry and Cadence Blake's daughter and figure out who Chelsea really was."

She hammered another nail in a little harder than the previous ones.

"I take it they weren't happy with your decision?"

"I was supposed to end up in management for one

of the biggest law firms in New York." She rolled her eyes. "Now I work for a temp agency, I live above my sister's photography studio, and I'm out here nailing boards. What do you think?"

Picturing Chelsea working for a law firm was impossible. And he had no idea Mom had used a temp agency to hire her. Yet he had a hard time imagining any parent being unhappy with how Chelsea had turned out.

He finished nailing in another board before speaking again. "You said they're coming to town tonight. Where are they coming from?"

"Sadly, I'm not even sure. Somewhere in Europe. Other than a month at Christmas when they go back to their home in New York, they're touring the world. I lost track a long time ago."

They worked together in silence for a while. Parker continued to consider what Chelsea said. The whole thing was sad. It'd be hard for a kid to grow up like that and not feel a sense of abandonment.

Chelsea, for the sixth or seventh time, gathered up her blonde hair and twisted it into a rope to get it out of her eyes. He understood why she'd want it out of the way. But when it flowed down like a waterfall to pool onto the wood at her knees as she bent over the dock… Parker's fingers itched to reach out and feel it. To run his fingers through the golden strands.

He squeezed the hammer tighter and tried to focus on his own work. His mind drifted to their argument on Monday.

*"I need this job more than you can imagine."*

She was right, he'd judged her without knowing all the facts. How many times had he been frustrated with people doing that very thing with him? The realization hit him hard in the chest.

*"I wish I knew what I've done to make you dislike me so much."*

If he could go back in time and change his behavior, he would do it in an instant. He didn't dislike her. If anything, he probably liked her a little too much. The fact was, in his old life, he'd have asked her out a long time ago. He'd have taken her out on a few dates, and they'd have gone their separate ways by now.

That wasn't what he wanted. All those short-term relationships had been empty. Meaningless. Just a way to pass the time and make him feel good about himself. And that included his relationship with Brenda. It'd taken his accident to make him realize how shallow his life had been.

He put another board in place and held it firm while Chelsea hammered in the nails.

"I think you're brave."

Chelsea paused, her eyes widening. "What?"

"It takes real courage to break away from everything you know and blaze a new trail all on your own. You should be proud of yourself." Parker reached out to a wavy bit of hair hanging by her cheek. He twirled it gently around one finger and tucked it behind her ear. He let his hand linger there, lightly brushing her neck when he pulled it back.

With a sharp inhale, Chelsea's hand holding the hammer drifted, resting on the dock. Her gaze followed it before those long eyelashes lifted. The depth in her eyes pulled Parker in and all sense of time disappeared.

Before he realized what he was doing, Parker leaned in until his lips brushed against hers. It was a whisper of a kiss, but the softness of her lips combined with the scent of her skin made him want to pull her into his arms.

Chelsea's phone chimed from her back pocket. She jerked as though she'd been stung, color flooding her cheeks. She ran a hand over her forehead and reached for the phone. Whatever the message was, it sure was consuming a lot of her attention. She cleared her throat. "It's my sister. Apparently, we're having dinner with my parents at seven." Her gaze shifted from the phone to the pond.

Was she thinking about her family? Or their kiss? Because maybe it barely qualified as a kiss, but his lips were still on fire from the contact. "You okay?"

"Yeah." Her eyes focused on him for a moment before she picked up the hammer, her emotions hidden behind a wall of determination. "We'd better get back to this." She attacked the project with a new level of focus.

Parker hoped it was stress because she knew she'd be seeing her parents in a few hours, and not because of their moment earlier.

A moment he shouldn't have allowed to happen. Except, even looking back now, he was completely powerless when it came to ignoring the pull she had on him. Did she regret their kiss? As much as he tried, he couldn't.

He enjoyed kissing Chelsea Blake. A lot.

~

Chelsea had been home almost an hour and she could still feel Parker's lips against hers. For crying out loud, they'd barely kissed, but her heart was still pounding harder than any hammering she'd done on that dock all afternoon. He'd totally taken her by surprise, too. The way he'd watched her with those eyes that changed color depending on his mood. As if she were the only thing he wanted to see.

And he'd listened. Truly listened. She'd never revealed that much about her past to anyone except for Laurie.

The truth? She'd wanted him to kiss her then. She'd held her breath, knowing there was no way he would, but hoping anyway.

What she hadn't been prepared for was the range of emotions that'd pummeled her. Part of Chelsea had wanted to melt into his arms and have him *really* kiss her. The other part of her knew it would be a mistake.

But why had he kissed her? Did he feel something for her, or was he as caught up in the moment as she'd been? What if he regretted the whole thing? Anxiety gripped her heart. She couldn't risk her job. She especially needed to stay gainfully employed now that her parents were in town. Chelsea knew she'd get an earful about what she was doing with her life. Being unemployed would *not* enter into the mix.

And if Parker became any more to her than an employer, things were bound to blow up in her face. Goodness knows she'd argued with him as often as they'd had polite conversations. They'd gotten along for a whole four days now, the other shoe was about to drop.

Chelsea rolled her eyes as she checked her reflection in the mirror. Everyone else was at the hospital right now meeting Nicholas before going to one of the restaurants downtown for dinner. Her parents had already made the reservation. The place was well known for its amazing food and high prices. Prices for a meal that neither she — nor Tuck and Laurie — could normally afford. Was it wrong to hope Mom and Dad paid for the meal?

After staring at her closet for way longer than was necessary, Chelsea had almost chosen one of her fancy dresses she used to wear back in New York, but she'd hung it on the rod again. Everything else about her life had changed, why give her parents any illusion it hadn't? She chose a nice pair of black slacks and a peach-colored, long-sleeved blouse. She almost always got compliments when she wore it and she needed that encouragement going into dinner tonight.

Chelsea said a prayer for Laurie. No matter how nervous Chelsea was, Laurie would be the one who spent the most time with their parents. She didn't envy her sister one tiny bit right now.

Everyone else was waiting for her when she walked into the lobby of the restaurant. Laurie gave her a smile, grabbed her arm, and pulled her to the group.

"Chelsea, it's good to see you." Mom put a hand on each of Chelsea's arms and kissed both cheeks. "The peach blouse is an interesting choice. I've told you how nice you look in bolder colors, haven't I?"

"Yes, you have." Mom had her head turned expectantly, and Chelsea kissed her cheek. "You are beautiful, Mom." Chelsea was always amazed by how her mother never changed. Seriously, she hadn't aged in ten years. It was as if time had no effect on her.

Her father, on the other hand, had aged a lot since they saw him at Christmas. But he had that same charisma that won over every businessman he ever spoke to. "Hi, Daddy."

"Hello there, Chelsea." He gave her a proper hug, resting his chin on the top of her head for a moment before moving her at arm's length. "Have you been getting some sun?"

Mom stepped closer to peer at Chelsea's face. "Make sure you don't get too much sun. It'll cause freckles and you know men don't like a woman with freckles."

Chelsea's hand flew to her cheek and then to her hair. Could they really tell that she'd been spending quite a bit of time outside lately? Parker came to mind again, subsequently heating her face. But the conversation immediately moved from her to the waiter as they were escorted to their table. She caught Tuck raising an eyebrow at Laurie before his wife playfully elbowed him in the side.

They got to their table and sat. Chelsea noticed Laurie wince as she lowered herself. The incision from the C-section probably still hurt a great deal. Poor Laurie, she'd be a lot more comfortable at the hospital or her house. Or anywhere but here. And Tuck? That guy was a saint.

The group mulled over their menus and placed their orders before any real conversation began. Chelsea smiled. "Isn't Nicholas precious?"

Dad grinned then. "My grandson is a handsome little guy. He has the Blake nose. Don't you think he has the Blake nose, my dear?" He put an arm across Mom's chair and practically beamed.

Mom took a sip of her water. "I do believe he does. Such a tiny thing, though." She dabbed at her mouth with a cloth napkin. "I think you should consider formula, Laurie. It will help him to gain weight much more quickly."

If Laurie clenched her jaw any tighter, Chelsea was certain they'd hear teeth cracking any minute now. Laurie had texted her several times during this last week and the pediatrician was thrilled with Nicholas and his weight gain. There was nothing wrong with giving a baby formula, but Nicholas was doing quite well on his mama's milk.

Tuck cleared his throat. "He's gaining weight wonderfully this week. The doctor is hoping he'll go home Monday or Tuesday." He reached for Laurie's hand and kissed her knuckles before cradling it in his own. "We can't wait to have him home with us."

As it was, Laurie was staying with Nicholas at the hospital through the night and Tuck was going home to take care of Rogue. During the day, the family stayed together. Chelsea knew they were hoping the baby would be home before Tuck had to return to work a week from Monday.

Chelsea's parents talked about Nicholas and how the red hair had come from a great aunt on their mother's side. Which then morphed into a conversation about distant aunts and cousins Chelsea never even knew.

It was a relief when the waiter brought their food to the table and they had something else to do. Chelsea accepted her ricotta and had to force herself to let it cool for a few minutes before eating. She'd been starving since before she got home and knew she should've had a snack. She'd been way too nervous to eat before.

When Dad started to tell them about their trek through Spain last month, Chelsea threw caution to the wind and took a bite anyway. A little pain was a welcome distraction about now.

Her phone chimed from her handbag on the floor next to her chair. She reached for it, shocked when she saw she'd received a text from Parker. Maybe there was some kind of emergency and she was needed at work. Yeah, a girl could hope.

Mom and Dad hadn't even noticed she was checking her phone. She opened the text.

"How's it going? You surviving?"

Chelsea resisted the urge to roll her eyes. She texted him back. "I'm kind of wishing it were possible to drown in my ricotta right now."

Now Mom was telling them about how she could hardly wait until they began their tour of Ireland when they left the States again. They originally said they'd stay local for a couple of months, but Chelsea would believe that when she saw it. Mom was made to travel.

Another ping. "I knew I should've had you sand the dock to better prepare you to face your foe, Chelsea-san."

Chelsea tried to muffle a laugh with her napkin but didn't quite succeed. All four pairs of eyes were on her. She calmly wiped her mouth, laid the napkin across her lap, and covered with a drink. "I'm sorry. Please, Mom, do tell us about the hotel in Dublin you can't wait to see."

That was all it took, and Mom was happily reciting all the information she'd read about online.

Chelsea discretely responded to the text. "I fear the only battle I'll face is one of words, Mr. Miyagi."

She turned the phone volume off. The last thing she needed was Mom or Dad asking her any questions. Laurie caught her eye and raised a brow.

Chelsea gave a little shrug but couldn't quite keep the smile from her lips. That twinkle in Laurie's eye told Chelsea she would have some explaining to do.

An hour later, Laurie took a glimpse of the clock on the wall. "Mom, Dad. I'm sorry, but we're going to have to get back to the hospital soon. Nicholas will be ready to eat."

"You need to let the nurses care for him. That's what they're there for." Mom dabbed her mouth with a napkin. "I think we could do with a round of drinks to finish the evening."

Laurie immediately shook her head. "I don't want the nurses to take care of him, Mom. I want to do that. After all, we won't have help twenty-four hours a day when he comes home."

Mom blinked at Laurie as though she'd spoken in a foreign language. "You have no idea how much work a baby can be. You'll change your mind and hire a nanny in a week. Mark my words."

Chelsea could barely contain her anger. Mom had no idea what it took to raise a baby, since she'd hired other people to do just that. How dare she imply she knew more about it than Laurie did?

Tuck set his glass down and spoke firmly. "Our son will need to be fed. Visiting hours will be over before long as well. And I can't go back to the house before telling my boy good night." He put his napkin on the table and hailed the waiter as the man walked by.

Chelsea wanted to pat her brother-in-law on the back for his major redirection skills.

The waiter returned with their check and Dad took it, slid a card into the leather case, and handed it right back.

*Thank you, God. That ricotta was good, but it wasn't $40.00 good.*

Laurie appeared more than relieved, too.

Once outside the restaurant, they said their goodbyes.

"Your father and I are hoping to sleep in tomorrow. Perhaps we could all get together for an early dinner?" Mom patted her hair, not that a single strand had come out of place all evening.

"Sure, Mom, that'll be fine." Laurie's voice was strained, her face pale, as she stifled a yawn. Tuck put a hand on her back. "Why don't you call me when you guys are up and we'll figure something out."

"That sounds lovely. Good night, darlings."

Their parents crossed the parking lot to the Mercedes Dad rented and drove out of sight.

Laurie's shoulders sank, and she leaned into Tuck. "And we have a month or two of this. Maybe, if I breastfeed in front of them, they'll shorten their stay."

Tuck laughed loudly at that. "Honey, you did great tonight. I'm proud of you. Now let's get you back so you can feed Nicholas and get some much-needed rest."

"Yes, please." Laurie straightened and walked to Chelsea, hugging her tight. "Thanks for being here, Chels. Couldn't have done it without you."

"We survived, girl. We've got this. You go rest, okay? Call me in the morning."

"I will." Laurie poked Chelsea in the shoulder. "And don't think I'm going to let you get away without telling me about what was so funny earlier."

Chelsea suppressed a chuckle.

Tuck gave Chelsea a hug. "Be careful going home. Call us if you need anything."

"You bet. Good night, you two."

Chelsea got into her car and let out a slow sigh of relief. Well, she'd managed to get through tonight with no topics coming up that concerned her, where she lived, or what she was doing with her life. She wanted to count it a win, but she knew full well the whole storm was looming on the horizon.

She turned her phone on again and read over the texts from Parker. He'd sent one more that she hadn't seen before.

"Then be strong and don't let negative words steal that smile."

His own words brought out the very smile he spoke of. She groaned and let her head fall back against the headrest of her seat.

Her parents' thoughtless comments to Laurie tonight only made Chelsea more determined to show them she was creating a life — an identity — of her own. She would meet them again tomorrow and knew the inquisition would begin then. Before they left the country again, she wanted to tell them she had a full-time, permanent position at the ranch.

She thought about that kiss on the dock and how she couldn't wait to see Parker on Monday. She was going to text him back but changed her mind. Her job there was incredibly important, and she needed to draw a line in the sand. No, she needed to build a brick wall. And texting back and forth with her handsome employer was out of the question.

Handsome? She meant annoying. Rude. Outspoken.

The guy who went to visit children at the hospital every Monday.

Who bought her blueberry tea to apologize for jumping to conclusions.

Whose touch sent her heart rate to the moon and back.

Oh yeah, this was going to be way easier said than done.

# Chapter Twelve

P arker checked his phone one last time before switching off the bedside light. He'd hoped Chelsea might text and tell him how her evening went. He'd gone back and forth about whether he should've texted her at all. But as soon as he remembered how stressed she was and how much the dinner weighed on her, he'd had to.

But now he was worried he'd pushed it with that last message. Had he made her uncomfortable? He should've stuck with *The Karate Kid* references. Even if her smile was the first thing he saw every time he closed his eyes.

Happy made his two circular passes at the foot of the bed before lying down at his owner's feet.

For the first time in a year, Parker didn't dread going to sleep because of the impending nightmares. Instead, he looked forward to the weekend and even more so for Monday when he'd see Chelsea again.

Without warning, Kara's voice came to mind.

*"Why don't we pray anymore, Parker?"*

Because they'd gotten out of the habit. Because, in a way, Parker had blamed God for Dad's death. Or maybe it was more of a disconnect that he'd felt at the time. He truly didn't even know.

But his accident? He'd blamed God for that one. Blamed Him for losing his job, the damage to his body, the lack of confidence he had in himself after all of that. Even for Brenda leaving him.

Except, what had his old life brought him? Certainly recognition among his peers. A lot of money. Women sought him out, to the point where he couldn't go somewhere without dealing with the crowds of admirers. He'd told himself it was all part of the job.

Now? He enjoyed his solitude. In fact, he appreciated that he could go places in town without being bothered.

And he certainly never would've met Chelsea with his previous lifestyle.

If it hadn't been for the injuries he'd sustained in the accident, he'd have gone right back to roping. His heart squeezed.

"Father, I've doubted Your goodness for a long time now. I'm not even sure how to pray anymore."

Happy must've sensed the change in his owner's mood. He moved and lay down in the crook of Parker's arm. Parker scratched the dog's ear as he drifted back to sleep.

"I can't begin to understand why things have happened the way they have. I still miss Dad." His voice cracked. "He'd be happy I'm back on the ranch again. Help me to see the positive side of things more and be thankful for what I do have."

They were the last words Parker spoke as sleep claimed him. For the first night in a long time, he didn't dream about accidents or injuries, of fire or death, or even of roping or moments with Dad. Instead, it was a sleep filled with peace and the occasional smile of a woman with stunning green eyes.

~

Chelsea stood at the window in the hospital room Laurie had been staying in with Nicholas. It was a chilly Saturday but you wouldn't know it from the inside. Sunshine and blue skies gave the illusion of a warm day. All the bare trees would begin to get new leaves soon. Chelsea couldn't wait — spring was her favorite time of the year.

"Okay, spill."

Chelsea turned. Laurie had finished feeding Nicholas and was gently burping him against her shoulder. "What are you talking about?"

Laurie shook her head in mock pity. "I gave you time to tell me about last night on your own. But since you won't, I have to ask. What text did you get at dinner that was so funny?"

Chelsea tried to keep any reactions at bay but she couldn't. Her face heated as her lips transformed into a silly smile. "It was just something my boss said. He knew I was worried about last night and was trying to make me laugh. It's a long story and not very interesting."

"I doubt that it's not interesting. He succeeded." Laurie was all curiosity now. "So, I take it you and Parker are getting along okay now?"

"For the moment, anyway." Chelsea shrugged,

hoping she appeared nonchalant. "He's my boss, Laurie."

"And you like him."

"Maybe. But does it matter? I need this job and I can't afford to risk it. Especially not right now."

Laurie took her time kissing her baby's sleeping face before placing him carefully in the little bed next to the one she was lounging on. Once he was settled and the oxygen tube arranged, she turned to Chelsea, determination filling her eyes.

"You let Mom and Dad dictate everything in your life until you came to Kitner. Everything. Don't you realize that's exactly what you're doing now, too? You're letting your fear of what they'll think about you and your job determine whether or not you pursue a relationship with Parker."

"Whoa, now." Chelsea held up both hands. "A handful of texts and a kiss does not equal a relationship."

"You *kissed*?!" The last word came out as a hiss when Laurie tried to lower her voice so she wouldn't wake up Nicholas. "How? What happened?"

There was nothing Chelsea could do now except tell Laurie about that afternoon on the dock. "You see what I mean? It barely counted as a kiss. He couldn't even stand being around me until last week."

"People change, Chels."

"Yeah." Right now, Chelsea's heart was in a tug-of-war between hope that Parker had changed, and doubts insisting it was a fluke and they'd only end up arguing like they had in the past. Those thoughts aside, how would Mrs. Wilson feel about her son being interested in one of her employees? She could almost picture Mrs. Wilson yelling her right off the ranch. "I can't risk it, Laurie. At least not while Mom and Dad are here. I need to keep some distance for a while."

By the look on Laurie's face, she obviously disagreed. Chelsea's heart did, too. But she had to be smart about this. Letting a silly crush on her boss impede her job would be foolhardy.

Their parents would be in town for a couple of months at most. She wasn't so lonely or desperate she couldn't wait until they left to see if there was anything between her and Parker. By then, they'd likely be back to not speaking to each other anyway.

Chelsea wasn't sure she'd actually convinced herself of that, but it helped. The most important thing was to put that kiss out of her mind. Because *that* couldn't happen again.

Laurie was watching Nicholas sleep, her face sad.

Chelsea moved to sit next to her on the bed. "What's wrong?"

"I wish we didn't have to meet Mom and Dad anywhere. I don't like leaving him here at the hospital. If I could, I'd stay right here until he gets to leave with us." A tear escaped and slid down her cheek.

Chelsea put an arm around her sister and gave her a hug. "I'm sorry. Did you call Lexi?"

Laurie sniffed. "That's the only thing that makes it better. She's going to come and volunteer in the nursery until we get back. The nurses here are great. But I do feel better knowing his Aunt Lexi is looking out for him while we're gone."

They smiled as Nicholas made sweet little noises in his sleep.

Chelsea knew having him stay here at the hospital had been hard on Tuck and Laurie. She closed her eyes. *God, please let him go home soon. Thank you for helping him get stronger every day.*

Tuck's boots announced his presence. He looked concerned when he saw Laurie's face but Chelsea gave him a thumb's up and he relaxed. "They'll be here any minute." He stepped to the side to allow his older sister, Lexi, into the room.

Laurie and Chelsea let out a collective sigh and stood.

Lexi went to the baby bed and softly stroked Nicholas's hand. "I'll keep this little guy company while you're gone. I have some of the milk you pumped in the nursery. But if he's not happy with that, I'll call you guys and you can come feed him yourself." Laurie nodded but didn't seem convinced. "I promise I'll call you over any little thing, okay?"

Laurie hugged her. "Thank you."

Lexi's face brightened. "Anything for my nephew. Oh, and my brother and sister, too, of course." She winked at them.

"Let's go meet them in the lobby," Tuck suggested. They agreed and filed out of the room.

Chelsea glanced back one last time as Lexi lightly touched the baby's head. She knew Lance and Lexi desperately wanted children. But Lexi's fight with ovarian cancer had resulted in a complete hysterectomy. The couple couldn't have children of their own. The last Chelsea had heard, they were going through classes to become licensed foster parents. She had no doubt they'd be a huge blessing to a child who needed a family.

Speaking of family, her parents were waiting for them in the hall. It was time for Chelsea to put her game face on. Round two: Commencing.

147

~

Parker settled around the dining room table with Mom, Kara, and Ben. It was weird to think soon, he wouldn't be eating meals with Kara every day. Thankfully, Kara and Ben would stay in Kitner so at least Parker would see his sister regularly. Still, it wouldn't be quite the same.

Lunch had been served. But before Parker reached for his fork, he cleared his throat. "Mom. Do you mind if I pray over the meal?"

Within moments, both women had tears in their eyes. Mom put her own fork down and folded her hands in her lap. "That'd be lovely, Parker. Thank you."

Parker fought down his own emotions. "Father, we thank You for this food we're about to eat. We thank You for our health and for Kara's upcoming wedding. We ask that You remind us daily of Your blessings. Amen."

The others echoed with their own "amen." The room was quiet, punctuated by a sniff or two.

They ate for a while, the conversation centered on wedding details. Ben filled them in on the latest travel details for the honeymoon: A trip to Cancun.

When there was a pause, Mom switched gears. "Chelsea's been working with us for two weeks now. How do you think she's fitting in?" She used her fork to lift the last bite of her salad.

Parker looked across the table at her. "She's doing well. I wasn't sure about her at first, but she's adjusted to the ranch and her position nicely." He paused. "I hadn't realized you'd hired her through a temp agency."

"I normally wouldn't have used one, except that Deloris highly recommended it. And you know her daughter, Pam, runs the agency. I figured it was worth the risk to try something new." Mom shrugged it off like it was no big deal.

Well, if she did know the mother of the daughter who ran the agency, Parker understood it all a little more. Normally, he couldn't imagine his mom using a temp agency for anything. It was all about contacts, she'd say. Then you were bound to hire someone who was more likely to do the job you were paying them to do.

"Well, it worked out, then."

"You have no objections to making her position a permanent one, then?" There was no missing the way Mom inspected him over the top of her water glass. He'd put up quite a fight about hiring anyone in the first place. And while he'd tried to hide how he felt when he'd first learned of Chelsea joining the staff there at the ranch, he was certain his mom could at least guess how unhappy he was with the decision. Now, the thought of Chelsea disappearing from his life made his chest ache.

"None." He tried for a relaxed, neutral tone, but wasn't sure he'd achieved that.

"Good." The half-smile on her face and the twinkle in her eye caught Parker off guard.

Could she tell he'd developed an interest in Chelsea? He hoped not. He'd done his best to shove those emotions down as far as he could. Except that it hadn't worked. Goodness knows he'd thought of her non-stop since they'd worked together at the stock pond. Since he'd kissed her.

Parker hoped she might text him today. The silence

left him wondering if he'd offended her. What if she didn't come back to work on Monday? Surely, if she'd come back after how horrible he was to her last week... He suppressed a groan as he pushed down a wave of panic.

Mom cleared her throat. "What are you up to today?"

Parker had originally planned on finishing up the dock. But the last thing he needed was to go back and lament about that kiss. Out of nowhere, he remembered this was the night Ray and the guys usually met for a game of basketball. It might be exactly what he needed to distract himself from Chelsea.

"I think I might go play basketball with the guys this afternoon. They usually stop somewhere and eat afterwards. I'll be home sometime this evening."

"That's wonderful!" Mom appeared pleased. "We won't expect you for dinner, then. Getting back out with your friends will be good for you."

Parker made a mental note to call Ray after lunch and make sure the group was still meeting. After a year of hounding Parker to return for the pickup games, he had a feeling Ray would jump at the chance to not only get Parker back, but to take full credit for it, too.

He'd dreaded the thought of seeing the guys again after his accident. It still made him nervous — he'd be lying if he said it didn't. But maybe it was time to quit hiding.

~

"You're working *where*?!"

Chelsea cringed against the horror on Mom's face. "For a temp agency. It's not as bad as it sounds. I've gotten a great job that way."

"What kind of work are you doing?" Dad's emotions were more in check, but even he didn't look happy about the news.

Chelsea sighed. Their early dinner hadn't even arrived yet and her parents were firing the heavy questions at her. Too bad she didn't drink — something alcoholic would be lovely right now. "I'm in charge of scheduling and bookkeeping for a large business."

Laurie tossed her a curious look, and Chelsea gave a subtle shake of her head. There was no way she was going to tell her parents where she worked. They'd either be horrified that she had anything to do with livestock, or they'd insist on speaking with Mrs. Wilson and getting her a promotion — some place away from the barn. Either way, it benefitted no one for Chelsea to give up the name of her employer.

The food arrived at that blessed moment. Chelsea wanted to tip the waiter for his timing alone. Now, hopefully Mom could focus on what was and wasn't good about the meal.

Unfortunately, as soon as they started eating their food, Dad initiated round two.

"Are you still living above Laurie's studio?"

"Yes. The situation is working out nicely."

Laurie jumped into the conversation. "It's great that the apartment is being used. And Chelsea is a huge help in the studio. Plus, she keeps an eye on it after hours."

Laurie and Chelsea exchanged a glance. Their parents knew that the studio had been broken into some time ago, but they didn't have all the details. It was common knowledge the studio wasn't in the best part of town. Chelsea was fine there, though, and the reduced rent suited her well. Besides, having a brother-in-law who was a police officer in town helped a lot, too.

Dad jabbed his fork at her. "Your mother and I have waited for you to come to your senses and return to New York. But choosing to work for a temp agency only illustrates how much you've floundered." He put his fork down and gave her one of the expressions that got him just about anything he needed in the business world. "We insist you go back home. I can speak with the firm. You may have to go in as an intern again, but there will be a place for you. We can rent you a studio apartment if you don't want to commute across town."

"Yes, Chelsea." Mom folded her hands together. "Enough of this phase you're in. No more living in that filthy little apartment or working for a temp agency." The last two words were spit out as though they'd left a bad taste in her mouth.

Tuck held up a hand. "Now, Laurie did fine there. Chelsea has my number and there's been no trouble on that street for a long time."

His objections went completely unnoticed as though he hadn't spoken a word.

Chelsea tuned out the sounds of her parents' voices as they tried to convince her how foolhardy it was to stay here in Kitner. That it had worked out okay with Laurie, but she was married. Chelsea was alone. And there was no guaranteeing she'd find herself a husband with the kind of job she had.

Any hunger Chelsea had for her meal dissipated. "Stop!" Several other people in the restaurant cast furtive glances in their direction. She lowered her voice. "I decided to move to Kitner and I stand by it. I'm happy here. Since you and Mom are gone so much, it's nice to be close to Laurie."

Dad shook his head slowly. "Your moving here was a mistake. You and your sister are very different."

Chelsea was confused by his response. "What do you mean?"

"Laurie's independent. She always has been. But you. You've needed more guidance since you were a child. If it weren't for the schedule we set up for you... Let's just say we knew you'd need help graduating from high school and then college. It's all lead to where you are now." It was said matter-of-factly, but he might as well have reached out and punched Chelsea. "We laid everything out — made sure you had a good career ahead of you. And you're throwing away all of that time and money. Have you no respect for your parents or what we've done for you?"

They really thought so little of her? Chelsea swallowed back the tears that threatened to flood her eyes. "I don't want to talk about this anymore. Why don't we finish our dinner?"

Although, at this point, she doubted she'd be able to eat another bite.

Mom and Dad both focused on their food, but the glares they shot her across the table told her the topic was far from forgotten.

Apparently, as far as her parents were concerned, all her hard work had yet to prove she was an adult and perfectly capable of leading a successful life.

Her chest ached and she was suddenly cold.

Nothing ever changed.

# Chapter Thirteen

Parker pulled the sleeves of his sweatshirt down over his arms. He waved over his shoulder at one of the guys he'd played basketball with as he and Ray walked to their cars parked at the back of the gym's parking lot.

"You didn't do too bad considering you're out of shape." Ray jabbed him with an elbow.

Parker put a hand protectively over his ribs. "Thanks, I think. It was fun. I didn't realize how much I'd missed it."

"You coming back next weekend?"

"I might." Truthfully, Parker hadn't quite decided. He'd expected a ton of questions from the guys, but they'd welcomed him back as though it'd only been two weeks instead of a year since he'd last attended a pickup game. The several new guys were friendly, too. They'd taken in his scars with the usual amount of curiosity, but once that had passed, they didn't seem to notice them. Maybe hiding out in his apartment for so long had been the wrong thing to do. But even a month ago, he wouldn't have been able to entertain getting back out like this.

It felt good.

"Who's the girl?"

Ray's question caught Parker completely off guard. He quit walking. "What?"

"This big turnaround. Coming to the gym and actually laughing at my lame jokes again. There's a new woman in your life. Who is she?"

"Is that your new hobby? Inventing girlfriends for your single pals?" But the dubious expression on Ray's face told Parker he wasn't buying the attempt at redirection. "Mom hired someone on at the ranch a couple of weeks ago." He shrugged. What else was there to say? That it'd gotten to where he couldn't get her out of his head? That he anticipated the moments he got to spend with her? That he'd kissed her out on the dock? He wasn't about to admit any of that. Because the fact was, he needed to push past all of that. He probably wasn't good boyfriend material, much less cut out to be a husband. And Chelsea deserved much better. His right arm ached, reminding him of all his shortcomings.

"And you like her." Ray wasn't going to let it go. "This is the first time I've seen you act like this when it comes to women. You shouldn't ignore it. And I know you," he pointed a finger at Parker, "You like to bury anything you don't feel like dealing with."

"If it becomes something I need to deal with, I'll be sure to let you know." Parker pegged his friend with his best "Don't mess with me" look. "I'll text you by the end of the week and let you know if I'm coming back on Saturday. All right?"

"Sounds good." Ray extended a hand and Parker

shook it. "Seriously, though. Don't miss out on a good thing with this girl because you're too stubborn." He paused. "It was good to see you here."

"You, too."

They got into their vehicles. Parker started his up and rubbed his hands together as he anticipated the warmer air from the heater. He'd expected the guys to go somewhere to eat. At least, that's what they used to do after playing basketball. But now, over half the guys were married or steadily seeing someone which meant they had somewhere to be after their games.

Unlike Parker. He'd told Mom he'd be gone. He had no one waiting for him to come home or wondering where he was. Well, he may as well find somewhere to eat. His stomach growled, reminding him he'd worked up quite an appetite.

He pulled into one of the little shopping centers in the area that had multiple restaurants. He was searching for somewhere to park when he recognized Chelsea coming out of a fancy seafood restaurant with a small group of people. Was that her family?

Uh, oh. By the expression on her face, it wasn't a good outing. Parker found a parking space and watched as she said goodbye to an older couple. Once they were gone, the redhead he'd seen in the picture with the baby hugged Chelsea before she and a tall man walked away. Chelsea stood on the sidewalk, looking lost. He ought to drive away. But he couldn't. Against his better judgment, he got out and headed her way. If there was even a chance he could take the sadness from her face, he had to give it a try.

~

Chelsea was pretty sure a bar fight would've been more fun than that early dinner with her parents. Good grief, she'd gone in prepared to hear about her poor choice of employment. But what her parents had said…

She'd gone years feeling neglected when it came to the amount of time their parents spent overseas away from them as children. Even now, as an adult, she resented it. Especially when it came time to call them and tell them about Laurie being in labor. Seriously, who didn't keep their phone handy in case their first grandchild made an early entrance into the world? She'd always felt like she and Laurie were missing out on something with Dad and Mom being gone so much.

But maybe the opposite was true. Perhaps, when they were away, it spared both Chelsea and Laurie the constant criticism. Maybe all their traveling was a blessing in disguise.

Right now, she was ready for them to leave again so she could test out her theory.

Chelsea crossed her arms in front of her. She'd left her coat in the car earlier, but the wind had picked up causing the temperature to drop at least ten degrees. She should've checked the weather. It must be a cold front; hopefully the last one before spring arrived.

She stepped off the curb toward her car when she noticed Parker striding across the parking lot. She stopped. What was he doing here?

"You okay?" He gently squeezed her shoulder and leaned down a little to get a better look at her.

Chelsea's hands flew to her face. Had she been crying? She didn't even realize it. Ugh! She swiped away the wetness and sniffed. "I'm fine. If you're going to eat in there, it's pretty packed."

Parker looked confused then took in the restaurant she just left and realization dawned. "I was going to stop and eat, but then I saw you. You seemed upset. Are things not going well with your parents?"

She didn't want to talk about it. Not with Parker, anyway. During the rest of the dinner-turned-attack, she'd become even more determined to keep her job and prove to her parents — to herself — that she wasn't a failure. Which meant she needed to keep an emotional distance from her employer. And that wasn't easy when he was standing there, his eyes brimming with concern. Her stomach rumbled and her head pounded.

"Didn't you eat?"

Chelsea grimaced. "It's pretty hard to eat when you're under fire."

"I'll buy you dinner. You can talk about it or not." He was watching her face, waiting for a response. "Your choice."

What Chelsea really wanted to do was go home, curl up in bed, and have a good cry. But she was hungry. And even though every part of her brain was telling her to reject his offer, her heart insisted it'd be good for her. "Have you eaten at Daisy Belle's Diner?"

"I don't think so."

"You won't find better comfort food. My car's over there. You following?"

He gave a firm nod. "Lead the way."

It was even windier by the time they got to the diner. Chelsea shrugged on her coat and was winding a scarf around her neck when Parker joined her. He took in the surrounding neighborhood, his face oddly neutral.

She knew what he was deliberating. She thought the

exact same thing the first time she'd seen it, too. "It's okay. You can say it. The street's a dump. But you won't find better home-cooked food away from home than Daisy's. And as a plus, I live just down there."

That brought a look of alarm. "You live nearby?"

"Above my sister's studio."

There'd been a lot of responses she'd half expected, but the concern wasn't one of them. It warmed her in a way the coat hadn't even come close to doing. "It's cold. Let's get inside."

A friendly chime announced their entrance. Almost instantly, Daisy was coming toward them. "Chelsea, dear. What are you doing out in this horrible wind? Come. Sit down, sit down. Are you cold? I have a great spot near one of the heater vents." The large woman's welcoming smile turned to Parker. Chelsea noticed that her gaze hovered on his scars for a moment before she seamlessly continued in her usual welcoming way.

"That'd be great, Daisy. Thank you." They followed her to a corner table and took a seat opposite each other. The heat from the vent above softly blew Chelsea's hair and she let out a sigh of relief. Yes, this was a good choice.

Daisy pulled a pad from the pocket of her bright pink apron. "What can I get you to start off with? Coffee? Hot tea?"

Parker picked up a menu and leafed through it. "I'll take a Coke, please, ma'am."

"I'll take a cup of coffee."

Daisy wrote that down. "You got it. Rough day?"

"Oh, yeah."

Daisy clicked her tongue and left to get their drinks.

Chelsea picked up her menu. She knew what she wanted to eat, but needed something to keep her distracted from the handsome man who'd tried to make sure she was okay. Not only that, but he'd followed her to one of the worst parts of town to have dinner at a little diner he'd never even heard of before. To top it all off, he was wearing a sweat suit and looked relaxed. A far cry from the normal jeans and button-up shirts or jackets he wore at the ranch.

"What's good here?" Parker lifted his gaze from the choices in front of him.

"Almost everything. I'd avoid the Cobb salad. And the shrimp. But besides that, you can't go wrong."

Daisy returned then, set their drinks down, and fished out her pad and pencil.

Chelsea spoke up first. "I'll take a big bowl of your chicken noodle soup. And bring some extra crackers if you could, please."

"You got it, honey." She jotted that down and turned to Parker. "How about you?"

"What would you suggest?"

"I can fry up a mean chicken fried chicken."

"Then I'll go with that."

"Coming right up!" Daisy bustled toward the kitchen.

Chelsea dumped two packets of sugar in her coffee, stirred it, and took a sip. Though she wasn't normally a coffee drinker, it hit the spot. Between the caffeine and the warm diner, some of the day's tension slowly left her body.

Parker took a drink of his Coke. "Should I ask about today?"

"Nothing much to tell. I've greatly disappointed my parents and can expect the lightning bolt to strike me down at any moment." She shrugged. "Nothing new since I jumped off their bandwagon."

"I've seen how hard you work. How much you care about your sister and her family. Your parents obviously don't know you very well."

His words were like a balm on her bruised heart. He was right. They didn't know her. Maybe they never had. Tears sprang to her eyes again, and she willed them to go away. She refused to cry in front of Parker again. Or Daisy, either, for goodness sake. The woman would pull up a chair and join them, insisting that Chelsea report all her troubles. Nope, that was not happening tonight. She massaged her temple and the pain pounding behind it. "I appreciate that. Thank you." She took another drink of her coffee. "I'll never treat my kids the way they do. I'm sure I'll make a whole slew of my own mistakes. But they will know I love them, I enjoy spending time with them, and that they are free to choose who they want to be." With that last part, she hit the table with her fist. Coffee sloshed over the side of her cup.

Chelsea and Parker moved to grab a napkin from the stack on the table at the same time. Their fingers brushed and they paused. Chelsea's pulse pounded in her ears. How did a simple touch from this man cause her thoughts to skitter in every direction?

Parker took her fingers lightly with his hand and used his other to pick up a napkin and dab at the coffee on the table. The nerve endings in Chelsea's fingers sent electrical sparks all the way through her body. Could he sense it? Was it possible he was reacting even close to the same way?

She withdrew her hand and immediately wished she hadn't. "Thank you." She finished cleaning up her spilled coffee.

"For what it's worth, I think you'd be a great mom.

The way you dote on your nephew and your determination to be a better parent than what you grew up with." Parker's voice trailed off. He appeared wistful for a moment before a sparkle came to his eye. "I've got a dock that needs staining on Monday. If you're in need of a little Mr. Miyagi-style therapy."

Chelsea laughed loudly at that, and it felt good. "You know, I may have to take you up on that." The memory of their kiss there made her neck hot. Going back probably wasn't the best idea. The thoughtful look on Parker's face suggested he was remembering the same thing. The air was heavy with what neither of them were willing to voice.

~

Parker hated that Chelsea seemed to be uncomfortable as they waited for their meal. He shouldn't have mentioned the dock. Now, conversation was forced. He wanted to address the kiss directly, but Daisy came by the table once to refill their drinks. When she wasn't doing that, she was hovering nearby.

If he could find a moment to speak to her privately... Just the thought had his stomach doing somersaults. What if his interest in her was completely one-sided?

Daisy returned then with their food. The chicken fried chicken he'd ordered nearly covered the large plate. A generous helping of mashed potatoes with gravy and corn completed the meal. It smelled delicious.

Chelsea thanked Daisy and immediately sipped at a spoonful of broth. She released a contented sigh and relaxed against her seat. "Now that's what I needed right there. Daisy's soup reminds me of one of my favorite nannies. She made the best soup I'd ever eaten. When I was sick, she always brought me a bowl. It never failed to make me feel better."

Parker smiled at her, relieved to have a change in topic. He was also thankful for these little insights into Chelsea and how it had been for her growing up.

He forced his attention from her face and took the first bite of his meal, confirming he'd be eating the entire thing. It just goes to show you shouldn't judge a book by its cover. He'd normally never come into this diner based on its location. But obviously, he'd been missing out on some good food.

They kept the conversation light. Mostly centered around the cold weather and the cattle. By the time they finished their meal, he was glad to find Chelsea had returned to her happy self. Daisy tried to convince them they should have dessert but they both declined.

"I should probably get home." Chelsea's voice held a hint of regret.

Parker could certainly relate. He didn't want to say goodbye. "I'll walk you back to your car." He paid for their meal, despite Chelsea's offer to pay for her own. Then he followed her out of the little diner. "You're right, the food there was great. I'll have to remember that." It didn't hurt that it was only a few doors down from where Chelsea lived.

She'd put her coat back on and was fiddling with the sleeve. "I appreciate dinner. Thank you. I'm sorry if I wasn't good company."

"You were fine." He walked beside her back to her car. "At least you don't have far to drive."

Chelsea chuckled. "It'd probably be faster to walk,

but I can't keep it parked in front of Daisy's." She shrugged. The awkwardness had returned. She was kicking at something invisible on the sidewalk.

Parker swallowed hard. "Look, about the other day at the pond. I hadn't planned to kiss you, but…"

"I know." She sighed, her breath morphed into a cloud of fog in front of her. "It was a mistake. I work for you, Parker. We can't…"

The kiss probably was a lapse in judgment, but no matter how hard he tried, he couldn't regret it for a second. Chelsea's gaze remained on her feet and Parker hooked a finger under her chin to raise her eyes to his. "It wasn't a mistake."

Her breath hitched, and she nervously ran her tongue across her bottom lip, which only drew Parker's attention to her mouth. The need to kiss her again — to hold her in his arms — was overwhelming. "Chelsea, I…"

Daisy burst through the door of her diner waving something in her hand. "Chelsea! Honey, you forgot your scarf."

Chelsea met his eyes and took a step backwards, away from his hand. Away from him. "Thanks, Daisy." She gave the older woman a hug and took her scarf. "I'm going to need this."

Daisy gave them a happy wave before going back inside.

Parker peered at the darkening sky above them and forced back a groan of frustration. When he looked at Chelsea's face again, he could tell that the moment had passed. She was clutching the scarf like a lifeline. He steeled himself for what she was about to say.

"I can't do this." Her voice was so quiet, it was barely audible. Yet the words still managed to hit his heart with the force of a bullet.

"I've made some less than stellar choices lately. But when I'm around you, I want to be a better person." How could he get her to understand what was in his heart when he wasn't even sure of it himself?

Chelsea shook her head and moved a hand toward his cheek. Just before touching him, she pulled it back down again. "It's not that. Please believe me. I can't jeopardize this job. There's too much at stake right now with my parents here and Laurie needing my help." She pressed a finger to her temple. "I'm sorry." Her eyes begged him to understand.

He wanted to argue with her. Ask for clarification. Did that mean she felt something for him, too? If he weren't her employer, would she be responding differently? Every insecurity he'd experienced in the last year crashed into him like a tidal wave. He could almost feel the searing pain along his right side as his scars reminded him of who he was now.

Parker forced himself to give her a nod and then watched her get into her car for the short drive to her place. He waited until she was safely inside, casting one last look his way, before he got into his SUV.

The day had been packed with revelations, more than Parker could process. His mind and heart were full of confusing thoughts and emotions, completely overwhelming him. He let his forehead fall against the top of his steering wheel. "Okay, God. You brought Chelsea to the ranch for a reason. Knowing her has given me some direction in my life. And now this." He paused, grasping onto the one thing that echoed in his heart more than anything else. He was falling in love with Chelsea and the realization was both scary and exhilarating. "Please tell me you didn't bring her into my life only to have her leave again."

*Patience.*

Parker jolted upright. He hadn't heard the word so much as felt it, but it may as well have come from the seat next to him.

He'd been going through life on his own for a long time now and didn't have a lot to show for it. Maybe it was time to trust that God knew what He was doing.

Peace flooded Parker. He prayed for Chelsea and her family as he drove past the studio and headed home.

# Chapter Fourteen

When Chelsea's alarm woke her up on Monday morning, she had a hard time getting her eyes to focus. After all the crying she did last night, they were puffy and heavy. Just when she thought she'd cried herself out, Laurie had called to ask how she was doing and the waterworks started all over again.

She sat up and then let herself flop back down onto her bed, snuggling under the covers. Forget work. Forget the ranch. Maybe the whole thing was more trouble than it was worth. She closed her eyes and tried to fall back to sleep. Merely five minutes passed by before she heaved a sigh and sat up again.

Chelsea was too responsible for that. No matter how awkward it might be at work today, she had to go. She'd never simply not shown up for work in the past, and she wasn't about to start now.

Parker's face drifted to mind. Goosebumps peppered her arms like they had last night outside the diner. If Daisy hadn't interrupted them...

She'd wanted him to kiss her so badly, despite every alarm going off in her head to the contrary. If he'd gotten the chance, she had no doubt she'd have kissed him back.

Telling him she needed some distance had been one of the hardest things she'd ever had to do. The hurt in his eyes had only compounded the pain in her heart. How was she going to face him today?

There were no tears left, otherwise she'd be crying again.

Laurie had assured her everything would be fine. That she shouldn't let their parents drive her to this extreme. Deep down, Chelsea knew she was right. But it was impossible for her to push that aside. Especially when she wasn't sure whether what Parker felt for her was more than a fleeting interest. She couldn't afford to lose her job right now and then have it not work out between them. One way or another, she would prove to her parents she could be just as successful and independent as Laurie.

By the time she arrived at the ranch, she'd decided to eat lunch at her desk for the time being and try to focus on her work. When her cell phone pinged, Chelsea pulled it out of her pocket and read the text from Laurie.

"The pediatrician stopped by, and Nicholas is coming home with us this afternoon. Oh, Chelsea. This is the best day. God is so good!"

That was the kind of news Chelsea needed to turn her day around. Instead of focusing on her own issues, she planned on what she'd drop off at their house for dinner the following day. Tuck's whole family was coordinating to make sure the new family of three wouldn't have to cook for a week. Chelsea was thankful to be an extended part of the Chandler clan.

She managed to get through the week, which included another awkward dinner with her parents. The topic of her life and what she was doing with it never came up again. But Chelsea swore the temperature of the room dropped fifteen degrees while they were all together. It was fine by her. She'd take their stony silence over anything they might say.

Other than the notes waiting for her when she arrived at work, she didn't hear a thing from Parker. Truthfully, her days were long, lonely, and depressing. Even though her brain kept assuring her this was the right thing to do, it still hurt. She missed seeing him and spending time with him.

Chelsea had to finish a few things Friday evening and she was a little late leaving work. She'd just gathered her things and gone downstairs when she turned a corner and ran smack into a solid chest. "Oh!" Strong arms came out to steady her.

"You okay?"

Parker's voice did strange things to her heart. It was racing a mile a minute while simultaneously, she felt more at peace than she had all week.

She blinked as she looked up at him. "I'm sorry about that. I wasn't paying enough attention."

His hands lingered on her shoulders before letting them drop to his sides, his hazel eyes conflicted. "Well, I'm back sooner than I would normally be." Parker took his cell phone out. "I got a call from the hospital. One of the boys who's been there for weeks has gotten worse. He was asking to see Happy and they called me. I'm heading over there."

The poor guy seemed nervous. Before she could think things through and second guess herself, she trusted her initial reaction. "Would you like some company?"

His eyes widened before relief crossed his face. "I would. You want to follow me, that way you don't have to come back here afterwards?"

"Sure."

"I need to run and change clothes. Can I meet you in front of the house in ten minutes?"

She nodded and he left at a jog, Happy on his heels.

They made their way back to town and the hospital. Chelsea pulled into the parking spot next to Parker and got out. As they walked side by side to the entrance, Chelsea noticed that he was holding the handle of Happy's leash tightly enough to turn his knuckles white. He hadn't said a word, either.

"I hope the little boy's going to be okay."

He only nodded, his jaw clenched.

With no idea what to expect when they got to the pediatric ward, Chelsea prayed the entire way there. *Lord, I don't know how sick this little boy is. But I pray You give the doctors and nurses the knowledge they need to treat him.* She looked over at Parker as they rode the elevator to the second floor. *And give Parker peace and the words he needs when he goes in there.*

The elevator doors opened and a nurse waved them over. Parker reached for Happy and picked him up. "Thank you for coming, Parker. Kay left a note about you earlier." The nurse, with the name Camille on her badge, lowered her voice. "Norman's got double pneumonia. With his lowered immune system, this is dangerous. But he kept asking about Happy and wondering if you were coming back soon. His parents asked if there was any way to get you here early. They thought it might cheer him up a little."

Parker breathed deeply and gave a firm nod. "Certainly. Happy and I are glad to be here." He put a hand against Chelsea's lower back and introduced her.

Camille smiled at her. "I'm glad you could come as well. Let me show you to Norman's room."

Parker continued to hold Happy, and he seemed okay. But Chelsea could tell by the tightness in his jaw and the way he kept his eyes straight ahead that he was nervous.

The moment they stepped into the boy's room, all of that faded away.

A five-year-old boy was lying on the bed, numerous wires and tubes running from his body. He opened his eyes, saw Parker and Happy, and perked up.

A man and woman in the room, who Chelsea assumed were the boy's parents, lit up when their son did. The three were bystanders as Parker placed Happy on the bed. As if he understood the situation, Happy carefully lay down next to Norman, his tail wagging and his tongue going a mile a minute as he licked the boy's hand and face.

Parker sat down on the chair next to the bed. "You know what? Happy wanted to bring you one of his favorite bones. I had to tell him that boys don't like to chew on bones like dogs do."

Norman chuckled. He looked delighted, but the paleness of his skin, the dark circles under his eyes, and the sound of his coughs revealed how sick he was.

His mother came over to Chelsea, her hands clasped at her chest. "Norman always talks about Happy's visits. Parker's great with the kids. That he makes a point of coming here to visit them matters a lot."

Chelsea's heart welled with pride as Parker joked

and managed to get several good laughs out of Norman before the boy began to yawn. That's when he took his cue. "We'd better go and let you get some sleep, buddy. But we'll be back Monday night. I'm hoping, though, that you'll be feeling so much better you'll be home instead of here."

At that comment, Norman's face fell. "Then I won't get to see you and Happy again."

"Are you kidding? I'm giving your mom and dad my phone number. And when you're home, all they have to do is call me and I'll come visit."

"Happy, too?" Norman's eyes were hopeful.

Parker laughed. "Yes, Happy, too."

Norman gave him a thumbs up and yawned again. Parker ruffled his hair before picking Happy back up and stepping outside.

The boy's parents followed and the men shook hands. "Thanks for coming. It was important to Norman. To us."

Parker shuffled his feet. "I meant what I said about calling me when he's well and home again." He took a card out of his wallet and handed it to them. "You've got a special boy in there. We're praying for him."

"Thank you again." The couple put arms around each other and gave them watery smiles before going back in with their son.

~

Parker let out a relieved breath and strode for the elevator. When they got inside, he let himself lean against the wall. Every ounce of courage he had drained right out of him. He'd had no idea what he was going to say to Norman when he walked in there. The moment he saw how fragile the boy appeared, he'd almost lost it. But that wasn't what Norman needed. No matter how worried Parker was about Norman, seeing the boy smile and laugh made it all worthwhile.

"You were amazing in there," Chelsea said from a couple feet away as the elevator carried them back downstairs. "You made a big difference in Norman's life tonight." She reached over and rubbed Happy's ear. "You both did."

"Seeing him like that..." Parker shook his head. "No kid should have to be that sick." The elevator doors opened and he made a beeline for the exit. He needed the fresh air and sucked in a lungful once outside. Happy squirmed, and Parker set him back down on the pavement. For the first time since they'd left Norman's room, Parker let himself relax a little and turned to face Chelsea. "Thank you for coming with me. I needed that moral support."

She offered him a little smile. "You're welcome. I wouldn't have wanted to come alone, either." She shivered as a breeze blew through. It was getting dark now and the temperature was falling. "I'll be praying he recovers quickly. Will you do me a favor?"

Her request piqued his interest. "What's that?"

"If you get any kind of status updates on him, will you let me know? I'm going to be wondering and praying this weekend."

"Yeah. I'll text you." They walked in silence back to their vehicles. Parker opened his SUV door, and Happy jumped in.

He and Chelsea stood there, studying each other, for several breaths. He ought to say goodbye and let her get out of the cold. But after not seeing her for six excruciatingly long days, being with her now felt like a little slice of paradise. It'd been torture keeping his distance all week. He'd caught sight of her a handful of times, and with each, it was like fighting the current to go in the opposite direction.

Now that they were in the same place and talking, he didn't want to give that up. "Is there any chance I could buy you a hot chocolate?" He tipped his head toward a small coffee shop across the street. *Please say yes.*

Her eyes followed his to the neon red OPEN sign blinking through the gathering darkness. "Sure."

Parker got Happy set up with a blanket in the front seat and then escorted Chelsea inside. They both ordered a hot chocolate.

When Chelsea got hers, she cupped it in her hands. "I'm ready for spring. I've had enough of this cold weather."

"Me, too." Parker took a sip of his drink. The rich liquid warmed him almost instantly. "They have some good hot chocolate here. I'll have to remember this place."

Chelsea nodded her agreement. "So, what made you decide to take Happy to the hospital to visit kids in the first place?"

Parker set his cup down on the table and ran his fingernail along the edge of the cup sleeve. "When I was hospitalized after my accident, I wasn't positive about much of anything." That was an understatement. Early on, he'd been depressed. His career was over, but it hadn't totally sunk in yet. The pain of the injuries were so severe that at times, all he wanted to do was sleep, only to be assaulted by dreams of the accident itself.

Chelsea was watching him closely, as though his

thoughts could be seen on his face. He sat up straighter. "One day, a guy came through with his German shepherd. He was some kind of therapy dog and I guess they didn't normally do hospital visits. But they'd decided to that day. Seeing that dog... well, it put me in a better mood than I had been in a long time." He'd mindlessly peeled at the cup sleeve until he finally pulled it off the cup completely. "When I got out of the hospital, I decided that was something I wanted to do. I'd had Happy for a couple of years, and I knew he'd be great with this kind of thing. So we went through a series of classes. We've been going for about seven months now." He shrugged, his ears growing warm as he shared his story.

"It's great you're doing this. What drew you to the kids?" Chelsea had set her cup down, too, and kept her hands clasped together with her chin resting on them.

Parker hesitated to answer the question. But the softness in her eyes changed his mind. "They don't judge. Not like adults. They ask me about my scars all the time, but then, once they hear what happened, that's the end of it. I find it refreshing."

Chelsea nodded slowly. "That makes sense. It hurts when people don't see us for who we really are."

There was no doubting the sadness in her eyes. "Are things still not going well with your parents?"

She gave a half shrug. "I don't know why it always surprises me. You'd think I'd be used to it by now. You were right, though. My parents never knew me." She took a long drink. "I've always been their daughter and Laurie's sister. Never Chelsea. I'm not even sure *I* know who I really am."

"Well, I do." Parker reached across the table and cradled her hand in his. Not even the hot drink had warmed her skin after being outside. He covered it with his other hand. "You, Chelsea Blake, are a beautiful, intelligent woman. You never give up, no matter how many obstacles get in your way. You were willing to fly in the face of what your parents expected of you in order to find your own direction in this world." She was blushing furiously now, but he wasn't done. "And you were able to single-handedly drag a grumpy man out of his misery with a broken bottle of tea and your stubbornness."

Chelsea laughed then and covered her face with her hands. Her eyes brimmed with tears as she shook her head. "You're something else."

"Oh? A good something, or a bad something?" He hiked one eyebrow at her.

"Good." She peeked at him from beneath her lashes.

Someone else came into the coffee shop, bringing with him a blast of cool air. As much as Parker didn't want his time with Chelsea to end, he kept in mind the area of town she lived in. It was nearly dark, and he'd rather she got home sooner than later.

Chelsea sighed and reached for her coat, apparently realizing the same thing.

Parker escorted her to her car and held the door open. Chelsea started the engine and cranked the heat up all the way. Instead of retreating, he waited, one hand on the roof of the car and the other on top of the door.

She turned toward him, lifting her chin. "Thanks for the hot chocolate."

"You're welcome." He leaned down, his face inches from hers. "Chelsea?"

"Yeah?"

He placed a light kiss to the corner of her mouth. "I've missed you."

"I've missed you, too, Parker." Chelsea bit her lip.

It took all Parker had to give her some space, when what he wanted to do was hold her in his arms and kiss her until they were both breathless. "Good night. Be safe, okay?"

She nodded, closed the door, and eased out of the parking space.

Everything he told her in the coffee shop was true. But none of it mattered until she believed it herself. He prayed she would someday realize just how special she was.

# Chapter Fifteen

Chelsea was relieved when her parents insisted they wanted to spend some one-on-one time with Laurie and her family over the weekend. She'd done a lot of replaying her Friday evening with Parker in her head. Seeing him there with Norman had given her even more insight into who he was. As each piece was added to the puzzle, she became more and more in awe of Parker. Of his strength after his accident and the sweet way he helped those kids in the hospital every week. That wall he had up when she first met him was slowly crumbling. And every new view she had of who he was inside only made her want to get to know him more.

Now it was Monday morning and she'd seen him briefly, just enough to wave on her way up to her office. She'd kept busy with a list of things he'd left for her to do. At four in the afternoon, her cell phone rang. She was shocked it was Mrs. Wilson over at the ranch house. "This is Chelsea. Can I help you?"

"Hi, Chelsea. This is Mrs. Wilson. Would you have

time to stop by the house here in a few minutes? I wanted to talk to you about something."

"Absolutely. I'll be there at four fifteen."

"Wonderful. See you then."

The phone went quiet, and Chelsea continued to stare at the screen for several moments before putting the phone away. What on earth did Mrs. Wilson want to talk to her about? Was she not doing as good of a job as she thought she was? What if, with the awkwardness between she and Parker, they chose to let her go?

Blood rushed in her ears, and she fought the nausea building in her stomach. By the time she was walking up the steps to the front door of the ranch house, she'd convinced herself this was her last day of work. She'd just reached up to knock when the door swung open, startling her.

A woman a few years younger than Chelsea stopped short, a hand flying to her mouth. "Oh! I didn't realize anyone was here. I was in too much of a hurry. My brother's always teasing me about that." She held a hand out. "I'm Kara Wilson."

Realizing this was Parker's sister, Chelsea shook her hand. "Hi. I'm Chelsea Blake — I work for Mrs. Wilson and Parker. I understand congratulations are in order."

Kara beamed. "Yes, my fiancé and I are getting married on Saturday. I can hardly wait." The dreamy look on her face would've relayed her excitement if the tone of her voice hadn't already done so. "Do you have a meeting with Mom?"

"She asked me to come over."

"In that case, come on in. I'll show you to the sitting room. That's where she sees all our guests. It's one of her favorite rooms in the house."

Chelsea recalled the gorgeous fireplace and could understand why Mrs. Wilson favored it. She followed Kara into the house. There was an obvious resemblance between the two siblings. Both had the same color of brown hair and hazel eyes. But where Parker was tall, Kara was probably closer to five foot two.

They entered the sitting room where Mrs. Wilson was waiting. Parker walked in from the opposite direction. The two of them stopped. Chelsea was more convinced than ever that they were firing her.

Kara looked back and forth between them, her brows drawn together in confusion. "Chelsea and I ran into each other. I thought I'd bring her in."

Mrs. Wilson stood from the couch. "Of course. Thank you, Kara. Chelsea. Parker. Please, come have a seat."

From the wary expression on Parker's face, Mrs. Wilson had apparently called him to the meeting without telling him why. Chelsea chose a chair across from the couch while both mother and son sat on the couch itself.

Kara raised an eyebrow toward Parker. "I've got to run. Ben and I are going out to dinner. I'll see you later. It was nice to meet you, Chelsea."

"You, too."

Once Kara had left the room, Mrs. Wilson cleared her throat. "Thanks for coming over, Chelsea. I wanted to inform you we've been thrilled with how well you've done here at Wilson Ranch. We'd like to offer you a permanent position if that's something you're interested in."

*Seriously?!* Chelsea's relief was so great, it took

several heartbeats to realize she hadn't yet responded to the offer. "I'd love to continue working for you here at the ranch, Mrs. Wilson. Thank you."

"Wonderful!" Mrs. Wilson seemed genuinely pleased.

Would Parker be as happy about the decision? She tried not to flinch as she snuck a peek at him. The relief on his face spoke volumes. After the range of emotions and conversations they'd had over the last week, she hadn't known what to expect. Between not losing her job and Parker being happy about that, it felt like Chelsea could finally breathe freely again. She could tell her parents she was no longer working for a temp agency, but had a full-time, permanent job. This was a big step in the right direction. She'd start saving and maybe get a place of her own instead of living above the studio. Her thoughts raced around each other. *Thank you, God.*

"Now that we have that settled, I wanted to speak with you about something else." Mrs. Wilson pulled on the hem of her blouse to straighten it. "I'm glad you met Kara. She's marrying Ben Price this Saturday, as you know."

Chelsea nodded, not at all sure of where this was going. "It was great to meet her. I hope they'll be happy together." She looked to Parker, hoping for some clue. He offered a subtle shrug.

"Thank you. We are all excited about the event. Kara has dreamed of a large, traditional wedding for many years. It will take place at the O'Riley Country Club."

"That's a beautiful location." Chelsea knew the press would be all over the event. The O'Riley Country Club was elite, and she could imagine a full-page spread in the Kitner Daily Times. Having what would normally be a somewhat intimate event being the focus of the town sounded intimidating. Definitely not Chelsea's cup of tea.

Mrs. Wilson seemed pleased with her response. "Seeing as the wedding will be in the public eye and it's Kara's special day, it's imperative that Parker bring a guest with him to the wedding. This will be his first big public appearance since everything happened last year. I thought the two of you might attend together." She reached over and put a hand on Parker's, whose eyes widened as apparently he comprehended where this conversation was going. "Son, you told me you didn't want to go with a stranger. Since you and Chelsea have worked together for a while, I thought you might be more comfortable with this arrangement." She turned her attention to Chelsea. "And we would pay you for your time. You'd receive double your normal hourly rate for a full eight hours that day, regardless of how long you're at the wedding itself."

Chelsea stared at Mrs. Wilson. Wait. *What?* Her employer wanted Chelsea to go to her daughter's wedding with her son? There was no way on this planet she could've seen this coming. What was she supposed to say?

Parker spoke up from his spot on the couch. "Mom, I told you I didn't need you to find someone to go with me. Kara insists it's fine if I attend solo."

Mrs. Wilson didn't look convinced. "That may be. But you know the media will want to know what all you've been up to the last year. Things may have been quiet, but Kitner doesn't forget its rodeo heroes. You'll be questioned less if Chelsea comes along with you than if you show up solo." She motioned to Chelsea.

"If you've got plans for Saturday, we would certainly understand. But if not, would you consider attending with Parker?"

Plans? If she had any, it'd have to do with her parents. She'd rather stick a hot poker in her eye. But this? Parker was objecting to the suggestion. Was it because he wanted to go alone like he said, or because he'd rather not take *her*? How did Parker feel about the situation? He remained stoic, his emotions shuttered. How was she supposed to say no to this when Mrs. Wilson had just offered her permanent employment? "I don't believe I have plans. But I don't want to add any stress or awkwardness to the situation."

"Nonsense." Mrs. Wilson turned her attention to her son. "Parker?"

He opened his mouth to say something and then closed it again. He jumped to his feet and held his hands up in surrender. "You two decide what's going on. Just let me know where to be and when."

Parker excused himself as Mrs. Wilson went over some of the details with Chelsea. By the time everything was wrapped up, Chelsea's head was swimming.

She was being paid to go to a wedding as Parker's plus one. Talk about hitching awkward to a runaway bull and watching it disappear into the horizon. She still had no idea if Parker was happy she'd agreed to it, mad, or somewhere in between. This was absolute insanity.

~

Parker knew his mom well, but he hadn't seen that coming. The meeting had run the gamut of emotions. First, the hope when Mom offered Chelsea a permanent position followed closely by fear that Chelsea might turn it down. When she'd agreed, Parker had been so relieved that he took a full minute after his mom made her suggestion to fully register what she'd said.

There was no one else he'd rather take to his sister's wedding. And Chelsea had agreed. Except Mom was paying her to go. Had Chelsea agreed for the extra money or because she'd chosen to go with *him*?

Parker's heart sank. What if Chelsea had felt obligated? That was the last thing he wanted. He'd rather go alone and face Mom's disappointment than put Chelsea in a position like that.

He paced the driveway in front of the house until Chelsea came outside. She didn't see him at first, but stopped the moment she spotted him.

Nervous, Parker put his hands in his pockets before taking them back out again. "Hey."

"Hey." She blew out a lungful of air. "I can honestly say that was one of the strangest meetings I've ever been to." She laughed, but it was a nervous one. Her gaze kept moving from the bushes along the walk to the front door of the house and back to the driveway.

"I hope you know your job doesn't hinge on whether or not you go to this wedding." He wanted to pray that she'd agree to go anyway. But he stopped himself. *God, I'm done trying to control things.*

"I appreciate that." There was a flicker of relief on her face that was quickly replaced with doubt. "But Mrs. Wilson asked me for the favor and I don't mind." She sucked in a breath. "Unless you'd rather I not. I'm sure you'd prefer to go to the wedding with someone else." Her voice cracked and red painted her cheeks. She twisted some of her hair around an index finger.

"Do you want me to back out? I don't need the money. You say the word and I'll go in there and let her know."

Parker studied her face. Her eyes were like a mirror reflecting his own insecurity right back at him. "No, I don't want you to back out."

"Okay." Chelsea turned and walked toward her car.

He rushed forward, catching her arm and turning her back to face him. "Thank you, Chelsea." He moved his hand to her shoulder, gently squeezing it. "I was going to text you after I spoke with Mom. I got a call from Nurse Kay at the hospital. Norman is doing so much better than he was when we saw him on Friday. They said his improvements are amazing."

"Really?" The grin on Chelsea's face made her eyes light up. "I'm glad to hear that! Will you go back tonight?"

He nodded. "How's your nephew doing?"

"He's great. He's getting some chubby little legs. It's cute." Her expression had become so animated, it was contagious.

Parker visualized her holding the baby and that conjured up way too many images of a future together that he had no right to imagine. But the pangs of what could be hit him hard. "I'm glad he's doing well." He glanced at the front of the house and wanted to say more. But now wasn't the time. He reached out to touch her cheek but pulled his hand back again. "I'll see you at work tomorrow?"

"Tomorrow." She tilted her head a little, some hair falling in front of one eye. "Hey, I know your mom wouldn't have offered me the position if you hadn't put in a good word for me. I appreciate it."

"You're welcome. You deserve it."

~

Chelsea stood in front of her bed, the four fancy dresses she owned displayed across its surface. When she moved to Kitner, she'd gotten rid of almost everything she owned that spoke of her life in New York. But these four she'd kept, just in case. If someone had told her she'd need to wear one to a wedding that she'd be attending with her employer, she wouldn't have believed a word of it. She needed help.

She picked up her cell phone and dialed Laurie's number.

"Hey, Chelsea! What's going on?"

"I have to pick an employee of the bride dress."

"What?! Hold on a second." There was shuffling in the background before Laurie came back onto the line. "What on earth are you talking about?"

"Mrs. Wilson hired me permanently."

"That's fantastic, Chelsea! It's what you were hoping for."

Chelsea walked back and forth in front of the dresses. "And now she's paying me to go to her daughter's wedding with Parker. I'm supposed to give her a sample of my dress tomorrow so she can make sure Parker's suit matches it." The tone of her voice increased with each passing word. "How do I get myself into these situations? What on earth am I supposed to do?"

Tuck's voice sounded in the background on the other end of the connection. Laurie told him an abbreviated version of what was going on. "Chelsea? Are you sure this is something you want to do?"

"I'm not sure I have a choice. I mean, I do. Parker told me my job doesn't hinge on going to this shindig.

But really, how am I supposed to say no?"

"You realize that there's a strong possibility you'll end up on the news and in the papers."

Panic rose, and Chelsea tried to swallow it down. "I'm trying not to think about that."

"This is the first real social event Parker's been a part of since his accident. And he's going to his sister's wedding with a woman they don't know. It's going to be newsworthy."

"Oh no. No, no, no. Then Mom and Dad will see it. What will they say? I don't want them assuming I'm going back to the social circles I told them I wanted to escape. And I really don't want them questioning me about Parker. I'm getting paid to attend this thing, for crying out loud."

"It'll be okay. Have we ever been able to control what Mom and Dad say? There's no use in stressing out over that now. They were going to find out eventually."

Chelsea flopped onto the bed, her body laying across the dresses. "I know."

"Chels?"

"Yeah?"

"Put everything else aside. Forget that Mrs. Wilson is paying you. Forget about the news stuff or that Mom and Dad will find out. If none of those factors were in play, would you want to go to the wedding with Parker?"

Chelsea closed her eyes, attempting to slow her breathing and her heart rate. "Yes, I want to go with Parker." The words brought a measure of peace amidst the balls of nerves bouncing around in her stomach.

"You're falling in love with him, aren't you?" Laurie's question sounded breathless.

"I'm crazy, aren't I?"

"No, sweetie. Go to that wedding. Do you still have the dark green chiffon with the short sleeves?"

Chelsea sat again and picked up the dress that Laurie was referring to. It'd always been one of her favorites and one of the less flashy of the bunch. "Right here."

"Go with that one. It'll bring out your eyes."

"Thank you so much. Go back to your husband and that baby of yours. Give them a hug for me. And apologize to Tuck for my freak out, would you?"

Laurie chuckled. "Call me again if you need to. Everything's going to be okay. I'll come over and help you get ready on Saturday. I'm praying for you."

"Thanks, I sure could use it."

"Good night."

"Good night." Chelsea put her phone on the nightstand. She held the green dress up in front of her while standing before the mirror. The skirt went to just above her ankles. She couldn't even remember the last time she'd worn it. But Laurie was right: The green brought out the color in her eyes. Chelsea had never been one of those petite girls, but this dress suited her figure nicely. Crossing her fingers that it would still fit, she tried it on. Not only did it fit well, but she felt elegant. Pretty.

She twirled around, the skirt brushing against her legs. What would it be like to dance with Parker at the wedding? Would they even dance at all? Or was she supposed to make an appearance for the ceremony itself and disappear?

"Ugh!" Chelsea closed her eyes and let herself fall back onto her bed again. She was a mess. An absolute mess.

# Chapter Sixteen

It was Friday. Chelsea had only seen her parents once since the weekend, and the meal had been almost civil. All talk of jobs and living situations had been avoided. Which was good, except for the awkwardness that filled the room every time they were all together. She sensed there was something just under the surface that her parents weren't talking about. And that made her nervous. They were all going to Tuck and Laurie's house this evening for dinner. Chelsea was dreading it, though at least she'd get to hold her nephew. That always made things a little brighter.

She'd taken her dress over to the ranch house as Mrs. Wilson had requested. Chelsea and Laurie discussed hairstyles and settled on Chelsea wearing hers down, with a little pulled back to keep it off her face. At this point, she was as ready as she could be.

Her computer screen at work stared back at her. She had a list of invoices she was adding, but she couldn't focus on them. Her mind kept wandering to Parker instead. She'd only seen him briefly a handful of times this week. He had been running all over the place taking care of the ranch and helping with wedding stuff. At the same time, thanks to all of the rain this week, she'd been forced to eat in her office. So far, it'd been the week that refused to end.

Chelsea pushed away from the desk and stood to study the weather through the window. Thick, billowy clouds created a wall across the sky in the distance. Yet more rain was on the way. Claustrophobic, she went downstairs and stepped outside. She inhaled the scent of coming rain and sighed. She normally loved a good rainstorm, and it totally matched the stormy mix of emotions she was dealing with on the inside.

She crossed her arms and leaned against the side of the barn as the storm front slowly advanced.

Parker pulled up in his truck and got out, closely followed by Happy. "Good afternoon."

Chelsea smiled as he joined her. His elbow was an inch from hers and she shivered. "Hi. I had to come out and enjoy the smell of rain. Looks like our brief reprieve is about over."

"Yeah, it sure does." Happy nosed around in a bush. "Would you like to take a walk with me and Happy?" Parker nodded toward his dog. "He said he wouldn't go unless you came with us."

"Oh, did he, now?" She raised an eyebrow at him. "I wouldn't want to disappoint the poor guy. A walk sounds nice."

Parker grinned. "Good." He clapped his hands. "Come on, Happy."

They strolled in companionable silence for a while. Happy kept pace with them, his nose to the ground most of the time.

Chelsea turned her head to look at Parker. "Are you

ready for tomorrow? Is Kara excited or nervous?"

"I'm ready. I think we've been planning this wedding for years." He chuckled. "Kara's excited. She's practically fearless. She's been nervous only a handful of times in her life."

"That's a nice trait to have. I'm more on the opposite end of the spectrum. I was scared to try new things or do something I hadn't done before when I was a kid." Chelsea had often followed Laurie's initiative and took little of her own back then.

"Are you nervous about tomorrow?" Parker was watching her, curiosity and something else in his eyes.

"Very." She rubbed her hands down her pants leg and licked her dry lips. "I used to attend all sorts of big social events with my parents when I was a kid and even into my teens. I worried about whether I was dressed okay and made such an effort not to embarrass my family." She shook her head. "They were stressful."

Parker stopped walking. "I don't want you to feel that way about tomorrow. Even now, you can change your mind." He turned toward her. "No one will fault you for it."

Chelsea didn't even have to think about it. She shook her head. "If I could feed a treat to a longhorn, I can go to this event tomorrow." He laughed and she pointed a finger at him. "I'm serious. You have no idea how little I've had to do with animals."

"One of these days, I'll take you horseback riding again. I rather enjoyed it." His smile was mischievous.

She crossed her arms, but couldn't stop the grin coming to her face. "I had fun, too."

Lightning lit up the coming wall of clouds. Seconds later, thunder shook the ground. Happy ran back to them, leaning against his owner's leg.

Parker reached down and patted him. "That's approaching fast. Let's head back before we get caught up in it."

They turned around, walking back faster than they'd started out. It didn't take long before sporadic raindrops fell from the sky.

Chelsea giggled. "So much for not getting wet."

The path they'd followed curved ahead to where they could see the barn.

Parker took her hand in his and pulled her off path. "This way's faster."

It was raining harder now as they ran through the grass. At the wooden fence, he helped Chelsea climb over it and then followed her. Happy jumped over the lower rung and made it to the barn before the humans.

By the time Parker and Chelsea had ducked inside, both were laughing and more than a little wet. Chelsea shivered and looked behind them at the deluge. "Wow. You can't even see the fence. It's like a wall of water."

"Did you bring a jacket?"

"It's upstairs."

Before Chelsea knew it, he'd gone to her office and returned with the jacket. He draped it over her shoulders. His consideration warmed her more than the jacket ever could. She turned and began to say something when she noticed he had a hand over his right shoulder. "Is something wrong?"

"I snagged it on a nail when we were climbing the fence." He removed his hand to reveal a torn spot in his shirt with blood seeping into it. "There's a first aid kit in here somewhere." He went into the back room and rummaged around in a cabinet. "Ah, there it is." He retrieved the white box and set it down on the counter.

The red from the blood wasn't spreading too fast, but it still hurt Chelsea to see it. "That's more than a scratch, Parker. Here, let me help."

Parker shook his head, pink coloring his neck and traveling to his ears. "I've got this. I've had my tetanus shot, and I'm more than capable of slapping a bandage on a scratch." He took another look at the pouring rain. She suspected he might have tried to take the kit with him and leave if it'd been clear.

Why was he embarrassed? Or was it simply that he didn't want her to help him? Her hesitation and confusion must have shown on her face because his own expression softened.

"I'll be glad to accept help. But I'll warn you, it isn't pretty."

What wasn't pretty? She had no idea what he was talking about until he'd unbuttoned his shirt and shrugged it off. Chelsea noticed the white t-shirt underneath a split second before the line of scars that ran down to the elbow on his right arm. They were thicker and angrier than those on his face. The spot he'd injured was up near his shoulder, toward the back of his arm, and a small trail of blood was slowly making its way down.

Were the blemishes what he was worried about? Parker avoided meeting her eyes, busying himself with a package of gauze that didn't want to come open. He cleared his throat and craned his neck to see the wound and then held the gauze to it.

He was definitely self-conscious about the scars. She stepped forward. "Here, let me hold that. Do you have any alcohol in there or something to clean it with?" She put her hand over the gauze, her fingers brushing his. The heat from his skin seared her palm as the scents of pine and earth mingled. She didn't know if it was his deodorant or cologne or what, but she loved that combination. Her heart stuttered.

Parker pushed items around in the first aid kit until he found an alcohol pad. He tore it open and handed it to her. "How is it?"

She lifted the gauze and examined the wound. "You're right, it's just a scratch. The nail tore the skin, that's why it's bleeding so much." Her eyes traveled the length of his scars, her own arm aching in sympathy. "I'm sorry you had to go through all of that. I can't even imagine what it must've been like."

He paused his search for a bandage and looked at her. He seemed to struggle with whether he wanted to talk about it. His Adam's apple bobbed and finally he spoke. "A large truck ran a red light and hit my passenger side. They tell me I was trapped in the car for over an hour. I don't remember the accident." He shivered. "But I remember waking up in there, not knowing where I was."

"They had to use the jaws of life to cut you out, didn't they?"

Parker nodded. "I wouldn't wish it on my worst enemy."

"I'm sure it's not something you just get past."

"I had nightmares every night for a long time." Parker lifted a bandage and handed it to her. "Is that one big enough?"

"Yep, that'll do it." Chelsea cringed as she cleaned the wound with the alcohol pad. Parker never even flinched. "I think it'll be fine, though you may want to put some antibiotic cream on it for a few days."

"I will. Thanks."

They were both silent as she applied the bandage.

When she was done, she left her hand on his arm. It was so quiet, she could hear the blood rushing in her ears. She ran her hand down along the scars. "Do they still hurt?"

"Sometimes." Parker's deep voice rumbled near her ear as he turned to face her. "They're superficial. Ugly, but at least I didn't lose my arm. It could've been worse."

He was close enough now that she could feel his breath on her skin. She ought to put some distance between them. Excuse herself and get back to work. But her feet wouldn't obey. She inhaled slowly. "They aren't ugly, Parker. They're a badge. Proof you survived. That God gave you a second chance." She lifted her gaze to his, caught up in the emotions she saw there.

Her hand was still on his arm. He put his other arm around her waist and gently tugged her closer. A heartbeat later, his lips were on hers as warmth and contentment flowed through Chelsea. The kiss morphed from slow and sweet to something more urgent. Her hand moved up his shoulder to the back of his neck, her fingers burying themselves in his hair. He broke the kiss, his breathing ragged.

Chelsea's legs were weak, her pulse racing. Simultaneously, they both took a small step away from each other. "Parker, I..." But what was she going to say? That she was scared? That he was her employer and they shouldn't have kissed like that? That she wished the kiss hadn't ended?

Parker shook his head, his eyes willing her to not say a thing. He caressed her jaw with the back of his fingers. "I'll pick you up at your place tomorrow at noon."

She nodded, and he walked out into the rain and got back in his truck, Happy at his side. As soon as they were out of sight, she leaned her back against the counter. Her lips tingled from the kiss, and she could still feel his arm around her.

Going to the wedding with him wasn't going to be easy.

With a groan, she pushed away from the counter, threw the trash in the wastebasket, and headed back upstairs. No matter how many nerves and worries chased each other around in her mind, she couldn't stop the grin on her face.

Parker had kissed her. The kind of kiss that curled her toes and made a girl start wishing for a happily ever after.

~

The sun had gone down and Parker was lounging on the couch in the sitting room Friday evening, his eyes on the flames as they danced in the fireplace. His day had been full as he'd completed things on Mom's to-do list before the wedding. And he'd gotten through it all, even if his mind had continuously replayed what happened in the barn with Chelsea earlier.

That kiss they'd shared and the way she'd felt in his arms... He could get used to that in a real hurry.

Ever since, his mind had come up with different things Chelsea might have said if he'd let her continue. But he knew in his gut she would protest, or find some reason for why he shouldn't have kissed her. Truthfully, he didn't want to hear it. Because, regardless, he was escorting her to Kara's wedding and he needed a clear head. He needed to walk Kara down the aisle without distraction and make it through the stress of the press being there.

After the wedding, he'd do what it took to convince Chelsea how much he cared.

The sound of footsteps on the floor brought his attention to the door. Kara entered, rubbing her arms with a sleepy expression on her face.

"Tomorrow's your big day. Can't sleep?"

Kara shook her head. She sat down on the couch next to Parker and held her hands out toward the fire. "I've got a million things going on in my mind right now. I know I should get some rest, but I'm too excited." She released a happy little sigh and let herself lean back against the couch.

Parker put an arm around her.

Kara poked him in the ribs. "It kind of stinks, you know."

"What does?"

"I feel like we finally got you back after all these years, and now I'm leaving." She nestled into the crook of his arm. A small sniff told Parker that she was, at the very least, on the verge of tears.

"Okay, no crying. Mom will kill me if you wake up with puffy eyes because you cried. You hear me?"

Kara chuckled and sniffed again. "Yeah, I hear you. And you're right — she totally would."

Parker kissed the top of her head. "Good. And neither of us are going anywhere. We'll see each other plenty. Family get togethers and all that."

Kara stilled. "Chelsea seems nice."

Okay. That came out of nowhere. "Yeah, she is."

"I saw the way you looked at her, big brother."

Parker leaned away from her and she sat up, her expression mischievous. "And how exactly did I look at her?"

"Pretty much the same way she was looking at you."

Was how he felt about Chelsea really that obvious? The thought unnerved him. But was there a chance that Chelsea felt the same way about him? Even the possibility made his pulse speed up. "You're seeing things, Kara."

"Maybe. Maybe not. All I'm saying is that it sure would be awesome if my future kids had some cousins to play with." She winked at him and chuckled. "I'd better go try and get some sleep. You should, too."

"I'll go to bed in a few minutes." Parker stood as she did and kissed her on the cheek. "See you in the morning. Sweet dreams."

"You, too." She disappeared into the darkened hallway.

His thoughts shifted to the events of the following day. There were so many emotions going through him when it came to the wedding that he didn't even know where to begin. He was nervous about walking Kara down the aisle, yet proud to be the one to do so. And Chelsea...

The crackling sounds from the fireplace grew quieter as the flames dwindled. He needed to get to bed, too. He looked forward to tomorrow and seeing the pretty blonde he'd fallen in love with.

# Chapter Seventeen

Chelsea relaxed against the couch in Tuck and Laurie's house Friday night. After everything that'd happened at the ranch earlier and with the wedding tomorrow, she'd had to force her attention on the family dinner. Every time conversation lulled, her mind drifted back to Parker.

The dinner Laurie served was wonderful and even their parents enjoyed the home-cooked meal Patty brought over earlier that day. Little Nicholas was sleeping in his daddy's arms, his face plumper since he'd been able to come home.

Chelsea thought Mom and Dad would want to hold him more now that he was off the oxygen, but their contact with the baby had been minimal. They seemed proud of the little guy, but content to watch him while someone else held him. It made Chelsea's heart hurt. She could only imagine how Laurie must feel about it.

Laurie and Tuck had just laid Nicholas down in his crib in their room and come back to the living room when Dad cleared his throat.

"We wanted to talk to you girls about something." He looked to Mom and she nodded. "We're thinking of continuing on to Ireland next week." He turned his attention to Chelsea. "And you are going to come with us."

Chelsea blinked at them. In all the years growing up, she and Laurie never traveled overseas with them. "What?" Laurie looked as confused as she was. "What are you talking about?"

"We're worried about you." Mom patted Chelsea's hand awkwardly. "We've tried talking to you, and you don't realize the position you've put yourself in." She shook her head as if she were pitying a small child. "You're working for a temp agency. And I don't care how much you try to talk up your apartment, no one should be living in that part of town. You need to come travel with us for a while. See what else the world has to offer. Dad has a lot of contacts in London. Your great aunt lives there, and we've already spoken with her. She's agreed that you can come and stay with her for a year or two."

Were they serious? Hadn't they been listening at all? She waited, certain one of them would laugh at their joke. But their serious expressions continued to bore into her.

That was it. She'd spent her life doing everything she could to make her parents happy. Maybe it was time she stood up for herself. Stood up for what she wanted in life, like her job and where she wanted to live. And Parker. Enough was enough.

"I don't work for a temp agency anymore. I got hired on permanently at a local cattle ranch as their coordinator."

Mom gasped and her eyes narrowed. "A cattle

ranch? It sounds like a filthy place to work." She turned to Dad as though she'd just heard about a death in the family. "How did this happen?"

Dad shook his head. He pointed to Chelsea. "You will come to Ireland with us, young lady. We didn't hire the best tutors and put you through college for you to be a ranch hand."

Chelsea leapt to her feet. "No, you didn't. You hired the best tutors and put me through college so you didn't have to deal with me yourself." The anger in her voice surprised even her. "I go to work wearing boots and jeans. I've walked through mud, fed longhorns, and seen how the wind can go through a field and remind me of ripples on the ocean. And you know what? I love every minute of it." She paced across the room and turned to face them again. "I hated college, Daddy. I never wanted to be a lawyer. But I kept thinking if I did everything you wanted me to do, that it'd make you proud of me." She paused and held her breath. *Please understand me. Just for once.* Dad's jaw stayed clenched, his eyes hard, while Mom stared at her as if Chelsea had grown a third eye. Chelsea's heart fell to her feet and she swallowed down the lump in her throat. "I don't suppose there's really anything I can do that would accomplish that, is there?"

Laurie squeezed Tuck's hand before rising from her seat and joining Chelsea. "You guys didn't agree when I left to find my own way. But I did anyway and look where I am now. I have a husband who I love more than anything and a healthy son. I've turned my hobby into a job I enjoy." She hugged her sister. "You can't force Chelsea into your mold of a perfect daughter. You need to let her live her life and pursue her own dreams."

Chelsea's chin quivered, and she blinked away the moisture in her eyes. "For the first time in my life, I'm content with who I am. I'm happy here."

Mom held a hand to her chest, her eyes shining with unshed tears. "How can you do this to us? Both of you? Do you not care about your father and I?"

"Of course we care, Mom." Laurie sniffed and wiped at her eyes. Tuck went to her and took her hand in his. "You both have traveled the world. It's always been what you've lived for, and we're glad you're content. We want you to be happy. But it is a choice that *you've* made."

Chelsea nodded. "We'll always be here when you come back to the States, our homes and hearts open. But we have our own choices to make and our own futures to explore. I can't be the person you want me to be. I realize that now. And I hope, someday, you'll understand that, too."

Mom planted her hands on her hips. "We'll never understand. Your father is offering to help you again and you throw it back in his face. How dare you disrespect him like that!"

Chelsea's hold on her emotions slipped and a tear escaped. "Why can't you understand? I don't want your money. Or my great aunt's attempt to help me fit back into a world in which I don't belong. All I want — all I've ever wanted — is for you to accept who I am and respect me as your daughter."

Mom was crying now. Dad jumped to his feet, pulling her along with him. "I don't know how we raised two such ungrateful children. If you think you can do it all on your own, then you're welcome to try." He pointed a finger at Chelsea. "Make all the decisions you want. But when you fail, we won't be there to bail you out. You want to do this on your own? You've got it." He put a protective arm around his wife. "We're leaving tomorrow. You both know how to reach us."

With that, they gathered their things and left without another word.

Chelsea and Laurie stared at the door as Tuck closed it behind them.

"They're just going to walk out on their kids? On their *grandson*?" Laurie was incredulous. She rubbed her upper arms. "What is wrong with them?"

Chelsea felt more relief than pain at the moment, but that's because it was just her. But Laurie... and poor Nicholas. Chelsea turned and hugged her sister. "I'm sorry. They shouldn't have taken this out on you. I'll call them and —"

Laurie leaned away and shook her head fiercely. "No, you won't. You saw them with Nicholas while they were here. They have no desire to get to know him." Her shoulders fell. "He'll see them at Christmas and that's it. They'll be strangers to him."

Tuck joined them and pulled them both into a hug. "Are you two okay? I don't even know what to say to this. Your parents have no idea what they're walking out on. I feel sorry for them." He kissed Laurie's cheek.

Laurie sniffed and wiped away the tears. "The three of us and your family, Tuck, will be enough for Nicholas."

"More than enough," Chelsea agreed, drying her own face. "You know I'm going to spoil that nephew of mine rotten, right?"

Laurie laughed, the tears fading. "I sure hope so."

Tuck let out a slow breath. "One of these days, your parents will realize what they're missing out on. They'll see the amazing women you both turned out to be *despite* how you were raised. I couldn't be more proud of either of you." Tuck motioned to the kitchen. "I'm pretty sure Grams sent a chocolate pie over with dinner for tomorrow. How about I get us all a slice?"

Laurie nodded and blew him a kiss. "Have I mentioned how much I love you?"

Tuck grinned then and disappeared into the kitchen.

Chelsea bumped her shoulder against Laurie's. "After all these years, I suppose that conversation was bound to take place. You know what? It was horrible. But in a way, it felt good."

"Yeah, it did, didn't it? I'm sorry for all they've put you through. Don't ever doubt yourself again, Chels."

Chelsea released a happy sigh.

Laurie ruffled her hair. "You know what this means, don't you?"

Chelsea shot her sister a look of mock annoyance as she tried to smooth her hair back into place. "What?"

"You're free to go chase that cowboy of yours."

Heat instantly traveled to Chelsea's face as an image of Parker came to mind. "My cowboy, huh?"

Laurie waggled her eyebrows and Chelsea erupted in laughter, her heart lighter than it had been in a long time.

~

Parker fixed the cuffs of his suit and adjusted the dark green tie his mother had given him. Apparently, she'd gotten a sample of Chelsea's dress to make sure the colors matched. No matter what the dress looked like, he was certain this color would be amazing on Chelsea.

He turned several times in front of the mirror, examining himself from all sides. It'd been some time since he'd worn a suit. It was insane that so much had changed in such a relatively short period of time.

And things would continue to change. After Dad's death, Parker had been the man in Kara's life. Maybe he wasn't there for her as much as he should've been. He could've done much more if he'd stayed and worked at the ranch. But their relationship had remained intact. Now she had another man who was her focus, and that was as it should be. Ben would be there to provide for her and protect her. When she was hurting or excited about something, she'd go to Ben first before coming to Parker. He was happy for her. But he was going to miss it.

He thought about what it would be like walking her down the aisle and blinked away the moisture gathering in his eyes. It ought to be Dad walking beside her. Parker had no doubt Dad would've been proud of his daughter. And he hoped Dad would be proud of him, too.

Parker swiped away a tear. It was better to shed a few now and keep them at bay during the wedding. Goodness knew Mom would be crying enough for all of them.

Well, he was as ready as he was going to be. It was time to go and pick up Chelsea.

As he pulled up in front of Capturing the Moments Photography, he immediately recognized the figure standing in the window. The moment Chelsea saw him, a smile brightened her face. It reminded Parker of one of those window displays at Christmas — the kind that leaves you no option but to stop and admire it.

How long had he been staring at her? His hand went

to the ignition, and he switched it off, climbing out of his SUV. As he approached the front door, Chelsea opened it and ushered him inside. He took in the floor-length dress that hugged and flowed perfectly. The shade of green brought out the color of her eyes in a way he hadn't thought possible.

He was so intent on memorizing everything about her appearance, that it was a full minute before he realized they weren't alone. The couple he'd seen her with outside the restaurant were watching them and the man cleared his throat. He was wearing a Kitner Police Department uniform, and she was holding a chubby baby in her arms.

Chelsea's cheeks turned pink. "I'm sorry. Parker, this is my sister, Laurie, her husband, Tuck, and my nephew, Nicholas. Guys, this is Parker Wilson."

Parker shook hands with them both and smiled at the baby. "He's adorable. Chelsea's shown me a couple of pictures of him. It looks like he's really growing."

Laurie beamed at him. "It's nice to finally meet you, Parker. We came to help Chelsea get ready this morning." She gave her sister a hug. "Have fun and call me later, okay?"

"I will." Chelsea kissed Nicholas on the cheek and gave Tuck a hug. "Thanks, guys."

Tuck dipped his chin at Parker. "Take care of her, now."

Parker shook hands with the man who stood several inches taller than himself. "Yes, sir, I will." Parker had every intention of keeping Chelsea in his sights, and he had a feeling no one messed with Tuck's family without facing serious consequences.

He and Chelsea exited the building. She gave a last wave behind her before letting him escort her to his vehicle. "I hope this dress is okay. I probably should've taken a photo of it and ran it by Mrs. Wilson first. I went with a more subtle color." The tone and speed at which she spoke revealed her nerves. "I'm sure someone else probably would've been better suited to go with you. It's been several years since I've been to an event even close to this."

Parker helped her into the passenger seat and paused before closing the door. "Chelsea?"

Her eyes widened as she looked at him.

"This dress couldn't be more perfect. You are positively breathtaking." Strangely satisfied with the rose tinge his words had painted on her cheeks, Parker closed the door.

He thought Chelsea might have questions for him during their ride to the country club, but she said nothing. He guessed it was due to nerves. His own kicked in as they pulled into the parking lot full of vehicles and people flooding to the building.

Parker walked around and offered a hand to help Chelsea out.

She adjusted the skirt of her dress. "Thank you. How's your arm? Is it okay?"

He flexed and relaxed it. "It's just fine. You must be some kind of a miracle worker."

Chelsea gave a little shrug. "All I did was put a bandage on it."

"I wasn't referring to your first aid skills." He winked at her, kissed the top of her hand, and gently placed it on his arm so he could escort her. The poor girl turned red and ducked her head, but not before he caught sight of the smile on her face.

They approached the large building used for events and gatherings. Everything looked like it was right out of the fairy tale movies Kara had watched as a kid. Photographers from the local newspaper had already set up right outside, taking photos of guests as they entered. Parker hurried through with a large group, hoping to keep the focus off them for as long as possible.

The moment they stepped onto the patio out back, he heard Chelsea inhale. She took in the poplar trees with trunks wrapped in white lights, white canopies covering the chairs lined up for the guests watching the ceremony, and bouquets of white and blue flowers tied perfectly with ribbon at the end of each row.

"This is incredible." Chelsea's words were barely above a whisper.

Parker squeezed her hand. The decorations paled in comparison to his date as far as he was concerned. He was about to steer Chelsea around a group of people when Mom approached them.

"Ah, good, you're here." Her focus turned to Chelsea. "You are beautiful, dear. That dress is a perfect choice for you." She hooked an arm through Chelsea's. "Let me show Miss Blake here to her seat. Kara needs you inside."

Chelsea's eyes widened. She tucked a wayward section of hair behind a delicate ear. Parker doubted anyone else detected the insecurity in her face. The woman kept herself together, and he admired that.

"Will you be okay, Chelsea?"

"I'm fine. Go. I'll be here after the ceremony."

It took only a moment to see she meant what she said. With a final nod, Parker headed inside in search of his baby sister. He was ushered right to her and found her wiping tears from her eyes. "What's the matter?"

"I miss Daddy." She sniffed and fanned at her face. "I didn't want Mom to see me cry about this."

He pulled her into a hug. "Shhhh. You know he's watching down from heaven, right? He's up there, that big crooked grin shining as bright as any star. He'll see his baby girl walk down the aisle today. I just wish he could be here to escort you. I know that's what you want more than anything."

Kara hiccupped and shook her head. "I do wish he were alive. But right now, I can't imagine anyone else walking me down the aisle." She straightened her back and smoothed the front of her dress. "You've always been more than just a brother to me. You've been my protector and my best friend."

Okay, now Parker was the one who was fighting back the sting of tears. "Kara, I…"

She put a hand over one of this. "You are one of the kindest men I know. Thank you for being here for me."

"I wouldn't be anywhere else." He hugged Kara again, praying silently that this marriage would lead to a happy life for her. "We don't have long to get you into position. You know how Mom is with her schedules." They both laughed as they wiped away their tears. "We'd better make sure you're ready to go."

Preparations were finished and it was time to walk Kara down the aisle. As the music played, they waited for her maid of honor and bridesmaids to precede her and, finally, the little flower girl.

"You ready for this?" Parker placed Kara's arm on his and squeezed it.

"You bet I am."

Parker focused on keeping pace to the music and not tripping over anything. Kara was radiant. Then they saw the groom standing ahead, eyes full of love for his bride-to-be.

What would it be like to be in that position? To love someone — and have her love him — enough to agree to eternity? What would it be like to be standing there and see her coming toward you down an aisle, ready to be your partner for life?

As if she were a lone jewel on a sandy beach, Chelsea stood out from the crowd. His gaze rested on her face. And as the ceremony continued, Chelsea's presence anchored him.

~

Chelsea released a contented sigh as the bride and groom shared their first kiss as a married couple. The ceremony had been beautiful and the bliss on Kara's face — she looked like a woman who had never been happier.

The crowd of guests stood to cheer for the couple as they headed back down the aisle together. Someone stepped into the space beside Chelsea, and she knew without checking that it was Parker. "It was a beautiful ceremony. You did great out there. I would've tripped over my own feet."

"I doubt that." Parker's voice was so close, she could feel his breath on her hair.

"Oh, I would have. I did at my sister's wedding." The memory still mortified her, but now she could laugh at it. At least a little. "I was her bridesmaid and I stumbled. I managed to catch myself and didn't fall outright." Oh, it'd been horrible. But the ceremony had continued and her blunder wasn't the most memorable part of the day. Which was all that she could ask for.

Parker chuckled. "Well, I'm glad I didn't trip. I probably would've taken Kara down with me."

Chelsea giggle sounded nervous even to her ears. "What happens now?"

He glanced around the room and lowered his voice. "Well, I escort my mother and my date to the reception where I hope we can find something to eat."

She laughed as he held an arm out for her. Events of the ceremony continued full speed ahead. They enjoyed a fancy dinner and before she knew it, it was time for the dance.

Music began, and Ben gathered Kara close as he twirled her around the dance floor, never taking his eyes off his new bride. Members of the local press went crazy taking photos. The newly married couple didn't seem to even notice.

The rest of the guests were invited to join by dancing as well. Chelsea was content to sit on the sidelines, not at all keen on drawing attention to herself. But Parker stood and held a hand out to her. "I think we're obligated to dance at least once."

Chelsea glanced at the area where the media was lined up. Her breath seized and her face was suddenly hot. "I'm not sure that's a good idea."

Parker took in the situation. "I hate to tell you this, but they've been taking pictures of you all day."

Her eyes slid closed, and she groaned. Seriously? She thought she'd been flying under the radar.

Well, if there would be photos in the paper, she supposed one of her dancing was better than one of her gawking at the bride or dabbing her eyes as the ceremony ended. At least that's what she told herself.

With a slight nod of agreement, she placed her hand in his. Parker expertly swept her onto the dance floor as flashes from the photographers followed them. For the first time, Chelsea was really glad her parents had put her through all those dance lessons. She swayed with ease as she breathed in Parker's scent and slowly relaxed in his arms.

Before long, everything around Chelsea faded away, including the media. Nothing remained except for the sensations of being held by Parker and the movement as they danced.

She'd been to plenty of fancy dances — more than she could count. But right now, with this dress, the music, the magic of the event, it was different. She'd run away from that life and had worked hard to try and make something of herself. Yet here she was, at an event she escaped from, and it felt like home. There could only be one reason for that: Parker.

The realization caused her to stumble, and Parker's arms closed around her even tighter, preventing her from falling.

"Hey, you okay?"

Chelsea didn't trust her voice. She nodded once.

He must have thought she was still nervous about the press. His thumb softly caressed her back as he spoke. "I'm sorry they make you uncomfortable. If it helps, I'm sure they're focusing on me. On my... my face."

Chelsea lifted her head. The uncertainty in his eyes went right to her heart. This was the first big public appearance since his accident. It had to make him uneasy, too. Her eyes took in the scars on the right side of his face, and the unmarred skin on the left. Together, they made the man that stood in front of her. As if her hand had a mind of its own, she lightly ran a single finger down the path on his cheek. "People will see what they want to see. Nothing you say or do can change that. But if they're focused on you, it's not because of your scars or your amazing dance moves." He smiled at that. "It's because they're getting glimpses of who you are."

Parker's mouth opened slightly, as though he were going to say something, and closed again. He cast a look around them, apparently remembering that they were in the public eye. He swallowed hard as he kept time to the rhythm of the music, his eyes a melting pot of emotions.

*Great, Chels. Apparently, you just stuck your foot in it. It's his sister's wedding. Why couldn't you keep your mouth shut?*

They'd made their way to the edge of the dance floor by the time the song came to an end. Parker took her hand and guided her through the door nearby and to the wrap around porch outside. White lights along the roof overhead twinkled in the dwindling daylight. Nearly everyone was inside celebrating, and they had the area to themselves.

Parker rested his hands on the railing and looked out over the garden on the other side. Was he upset? Chelsea used her hands to gather her hair at the base of her neck and bring it over her shoulder. "Parker? If I overstepped earlier, I apologize."

He whirled around to face her, taking two steps forward that put them toe to toe. "What you said before… I don't care about any of them or what they think when they see me. I only want to know one thing: What do *you* see?"

Chelsea raised a hand and gently touched his face. "A man who's fiercely loyal to his family. A man with a good heart who can swing a mean hammer." Parker chuckled. "But most of all, I see a man who is sweet, thoughtful, and handsome. And I was proud to be out there dancing with you tonight." His arms circled her waist, and he pulled her close. She tipped her head back to look at him. "I spent my life putting what *I* wanted on the back burner because I was hoping it'd make my parents happy. I didn't realize how much I was missing out on. I just needed to be me."

Parker smiled then, slowly moving them to the music that filtered out from the dance hall. "And who are you?"

"I'm a girl who enjoys being near her sister and plans to be a ridiculously doting aunt. I'm someone who works for a ranch and enjoys every minute of it, mud not included." She winked then and a chuckle rumbled from his chest. Chelsea took a deep breath. "And, despite all my intentions to the contrary, I've managed to fall for my boss."

Parker stopped moving then, his gaze caressing her face. "I'm glad. Because he's fallen head over heels for you, too." He lifted a hand and cupped her face, his thumb tracing her mouth. "I love you, Chelsea."

"I love you, too."

The white lights twinkled like fireflies as Parker's lips covered hers. Chelsea melted into his arms and together, they swayed to the music that flowed around them.

# Epilogue
## *Three Months Later*

Parker's eyes scanned the fence line for Chelsea and located her at the same time Happy did. The dog took off running, leaping like a rabbit through the tall grass. After all the rain they got in May, everything from the grass to the trees was green.

Chelsea tilted her head back and laughed when one of the longhorn calves on the other side of the fence let out a bellow. Happy stood his ground on his side for several moments before following a scent into a patch of brush.

"I figured I'd find you here." Parker wrapped his arms around Chelsea, gave her a kiss, and held her close. "How's the newest member of the herd doing?" He nodded toward a small, black heifer calf who was hungrily drinking milk from her mama.

Chelsea turned in his arms so she could look out over the herd. "Good." She leaned her head back against his chest.

"And how about you?" Parker kissed her neck until goosebumps appeared on her arms.

She giggled. "I'm better now."

"I'm glad. Me, too." Parker took her left hand in his and placed a kiss on the engagement ring he'd given her last week. The sun caught the small diamond, making it sparkle. "I heard from the realtor, and they accepted our offer." They'd driven by the sixty-acre spread several times before finally making the call. It might be small compared to his parents' ranch, but it was perfect. Between the small creek running through it, the stock pond, and an abundance of trees, Parker could easily imagine their future home nestled right in the middle.

Chelsea jumped around to face him, her arms circling around his neck. "Are you serious? We got it?"

"It's all ours."

She grinned, then stood on tip toes to reach his lips. He was more than happy to kiss her until they were both short of breath.

When he set her back down on her feet, she looked up with smiling eyes. "I can't wait to begin our lives together."

"Me, either." Parker kissed her. "But for now, we'd better hurry or we'll be late for dinner. Kara and Ben will be there."

They held hands and headed back toward the ranch house. As they neared the gravel road, Parker saw the water in the ditch alongside it. Without warning, he scooped Chelsea into his arms, entertained by the little squeak she made in response.

"What're you carrying me for?"

Parker nodded toward her stylish black boots. "Don't want you to get your feet muddy." He stepped across the mess and set her back down on the road. "One of these days, you're going to have to cave and buy yourself a pair of real cowgirl boots."

"If I do, will you still carry me over the mud puddles?" She stuck her lower lip out in a pout.

"Absolutely." Parker leaned in and captured that lip with a kiss. "Any excuse to get you in my arms." He liked that his comments still easily brought a blush to her cheeks.

Chelsea shook her head, hands on her hips. "Are you ever going to stop teasing me?"

"Nope."

"Good." Chelsea leaned close and laid her head against his shoulder. "I kinda like you, Parker Wilson."

Parker laughed loudly, put his arm around her, and kissed her forehead. "I don't know what I'd do without you, girl."

The intensity of the emotions made Parker's heart stutter. After his accident, he wasn't sure he'd ever find a true focus in his life again. And then he met Chelsea over a bottle of broken frou-frou tea. He'd had a feeling his life would change, but had no idea God would use her to bring true joy back into his life again.

A joy he had no intention of ever letting go again.

# Acknowledgments

I'm so incredibly thankful for my family. Doug, I couldn't write these books without your encouragement and support. You always listen to my ideas, provide input, and read everything I write. I appreciate you more than I could ever say. Xander and Sydney, you always bring a smile to my face and joy to my heart.

Crystal, I'm blessed to have you for a friend and a critique partner. Thank goodness for salt rock lamps, essential oils, tea, and editing chocolate. Welcome to the hippie life, my friend. Here's to the many more adventures we'll be embarking on in the future.

The members of my critique group are an incredible bunch of ladies. Vicki, Franky, and Rachel, thanks for everything you do. Your helpful insights and sharp eyes helped to hone this book into what it is now.

My books also wouldn't be the same if it weren't for my wonderful beta readers: Steph, Faith, Tammie, Kris, Denny, Sandy, Shanna, and Debbie. You ladies simply rock and I'm so thankful for you all!

Thank you, Jen and Richard, for helping me with my formatting issues for the paperback. You saved my sanity — seriously.

I want to send a special thank you to Justin, Diane,

and Jordan at the <u>Whining Bull Ranch</u>. I thoroughly enjoyed touring your wonderful place. Writing about Texas longhorns is one thing, but getting to see them in person, watch them run, and even feed them treats was an experience I won't forget. I hope my readers will get a sense of just how amazing these animals truly are.

Above all, I want to thank my heavenly Father for all that He's done in my life. Writing novels is something I'd always dreamed of doing, and I'm so grateful that He's turned that dream into a reality. I pray He takes this book and uses it for His glory.

# About the Author

Melanie D. Snitker has enjoyed writing fiction for as long as she can remember. She started out writing episodes of cartoon shows that she wanted to see as a child and her love of writing grew from there. She and her husband live in Texas with their two children who keep their lives full of adventure, and two dogs who add a dash of mischief to the family dynamics. In her spare time, Melanie enjoys photography, reading, crochet, baking, archery, camping and hanging out with family and friends.

http://www.melaniedsnitker.com
https://www.instagram.com/melaniedsnitker/
https://www.facebook.com/melaniedsnitker

# Books by Melanie D. Snitker

**Calming the Storm**

**Life Unexpected Complete Series**
Safe In His Arms
Someone to Trust
Starting Anew

**Love's Compass Complete Series**
Finding Peace
Finding Hope
Finding Courage
Finding Faith
Finding Joy
Finding Grace

**Brides of Clearwater**
Marrying Mandy
Marrying Raven
Marrying Chrissy

**Welcome to Romance**
Fall Into Romance
A Merry Miracle in Romance

Made in United States
Troutdale, OR
07/02/2025